# HONOR'S MOUNTAIN PROMISE

## HEARTS OF MONTANA
### BOOK FIVE

## MISTY M. BELLER

Misty M. Beller
BOOKS

Unless otherwise indicated, all Scripture quotations are taken from the Holy Bible, Kings James Version.

Cover design by Evelyne Labelle at Carpe Librum Book Design
www.carpelibrumbookdesign.com

ISBN-13 Trade Paperback: 978-1-954810-57-0

ISBN-13 Large Print Paperback: 978-1-954810-58-7

ISBN-13 Casebound Hardback: 978-1-954810-59-4

*He brought me up also out of an horrible pit,*
*    out of the miry clay,*
*and set my feet upon a rock, and established*
*    my goings.*

— PSALM 40:2 (KJV)

# CHAPTER 1

*a*aron Long tightened his hands around the mule team's reins as the dog halted in the trail ahead of them, ears pricked toward something in the distance. The mangy mutt's body nearly quivered with tension.

Aaron peered through the scattering of pines ahead, but no sign of movement flashed through the branches.

A low growl slipped from the dog's throat, and Aaron lifted the rifle from the seat beside him to firing position. "Who's there, Barney?" Of course, the mutt didn't answer.

Still no motion ahead. No sounds. In fact...nothing. Not the twitter of a bird or even the rustle of wind.

A shiver slid down Aaron's arms, and he shifted to

1

climb down from his freight wagon's bench. He kept tight hold of the bar he'd fastened for support until both his legs landed on the ground and his right leg secured its balance. Then he eased some of his weight onto the gimpy left limb, finally releasing the bar once he stood straight.

This leg might be the death of him yet. He'd survived the bullet that ripped away part of his thigh bone, then the surgery to add a metal plate to replace the missing fragments. Even endured the year of dark days as he recovered and learned to walk again. With God's help, he'd mostly come to peace about the accident—he'd been the one in the wrong after all—but the way this leg slowed him down still pressed on his frustrations. Not to mention the constant ache on cold days like today. With winter coming on, this pain would be his steady companion for months.

As he hobbled along the road, another burning in that limb made itself known, this one farther down. His shoe had rubbed a hole through his stocking and started into his flesh two days ago. He'd stopped to help a driver retrieve items from an overturned load, and all that walking up and down the mountainside had started a chafing that hadn't stopped since.

*We glory in tribulations also: knowing that tribulation worketh patience.* He replayed the verse from Romans that he'd been clinging to ever since he'd found those powerful words. According to the apostle Paul, patience would produce perseverance, and the perseverance would turn into hope. *Lord, I could use some hope right now.*

He pushed aside the pain and dark thoughts it always tried to summon, then stepped forward, focusing on the road ahead. Barney still held his position, staring into the distance, but occasionally the dog would glance back, as though to make sure Aaron was following.

Aaron did his best to quiet his footfalls as he limped forward, though he could never manage the silent stalk he'd mastered before—in his past life. The road wound through the trees, but he took a more direct route so he didn't have to walk as far. Also, the foliage would give him cover if a true threat lurked ahead.

Since he hadn't heard any unusual sounds, this was more likely to be an animal than a human, and the only creature this quiet who posed a danger would be a wildcat.

Aaron shifted his attention up to the trees ahead of him. Perhaps he should have taken the road instead of planting himself under so many branches where a cougar might be waiting. But the lower branches were far enough apart through here that he could see an animal long before he came close enough to be attacked.

Barney trotted beside him, just out of reach but never straying far. The mongrel probably only stayed with him for the food Aaron tossed him at each meal, for he'd never actually allowed Aaron to touch him.

Something dark through the trees ahead made him slow. That could be a boulder at the edge of the road, but the flash of color looked manmade. He shifted from trunk to trunk as he approached, resurrecting all the senses that had laid dormant so long now. He'd once possessed a well-honed ability to spot danger and move a step or two ahead of the threat.

As he reached the last tree at the edge of the road, he leaned around for a better view of what he'd glimpsed.

A wagon. Lying on its side, bundles and barrels spilling out from under an oilskin.

His gut clenched tighter. That kind of accident was a freighter's worst fear. One of them anyway. But where was the man? The mules were missing, too, so maybe the fellow had gone off to catch them. This looked like a runaway situation.

A glance down the road in both directions showed no one around, but just in case, he called out, "Anyone there?" He didn't want to be shot when he crossed to the rig.

No answer sounded. Only this deathly stillness.

Easing away from his cover, Aaron kept the butt of his rifle tucked against his shoulder, finger near the trigger so he could fire if danger reared its head. He wouldn't shoot a person. Not if he could help it. So many months of recovery had given him a healthy respect for the lasting effects of a split-second decision like that.

As he neared the wagon, he could better make out the smashed crates and spilled contents. Some kind of ore—probably silver or copper—meant this rig had been coming from one of the mining towns, headed to Fort Benton, where the containers would be loaded on a steamer bound for the States. Peeking out from the oilskin was the flash of color he'd seen through the trees. A carpet bag, stitched with roses and swirls that no respectable man would be caught carrying. The freighter must have had his wife on the bench with him.

*Lord, let neither of them be hurt.* He moved to the front of the rig and toed the straps that secured the team to the wooden traces. Ripped. This had definitely been a runaway.

Since Aaron hadn't seen a team of mules careening along the Mullan road, the animals must have split southward down the slope. Either that, or they'd turned and gone back the way they'd come.

He hobbled around to the other side of the box to see what condition the wheels were in. When the driver caught his animals, his next step would be to right this vehicle and try to patch it together enough to get to Helena, the closest town with a wainwright in these parts.

As he rounded the corner, a bit of brown in the grass caught his gaze.

*No.*

The pressure on his chest clamped down. *Please, Lord...*

But it was.

The fur overcoat...a tuft of graying hair protruding at one end of the form and two boot toes poking out at the other...

Aaron swallowed down the bile rising in his throat. *Lord, why?* A death like this felt so senseless.

He forced his feet forward. The man might not be dead, though his instincts told him it was true. Still...he had to check.

His weak leg protested as he lowered to a sitting position to reach the fellow's neck, and he wove two fingers through the growth of beard to feel a pulse. Nothing fluttered under his touch.

As he focused on any movement, a growl sounded from the road.

He jerked his gaze to where Barney stared. A rise in the road kept him from seeing what lay beyond.

A sound slipped through the air. Something like...breathing?

Aaron scrambled to push up to his feet, using his rifle like a cane as he found his balance.

The sound grew louder, like someone puffing as they climbed the hill. The driver's wife? His belly tightened. The last thing he wanted was to tell a woman her husband had passed.

He positioned his rifle at the ready, but not yet aimed, as he waited for the stranger to reveal herself.

A blonde head showed first, then the pretty face of a

female. Far younger than he would expect to be matched with this white-haired freighter.

As her shoulders came clear, she halted to scan the area. Those sounds had definitely been breathing, and they grew even louder now as she sucked in gulps of air.

The moment her gaze took in the wagon, her features crumpled. She scanned the rig lying on its side and the goods fallen out, her jaw slowly dropping open.

She still hadn't seen Aaron, so he shifted a little to catch her eye. He didn't want to startle her any more than she would be already.

Her gaze shot to him, her eyes widening and her jaw snapping shut. The moment her attention dipped to his rifle, he lowered it to point at the ground beside him.

"I won't hurt you, ma'am. I'm here to help."

She regarded him with a wary look. "Who are you? Where's Mr. Driscoll?"

Did she mean her husband? Or maybe she was simply a passenger he was carrying to Fort Benton. Aaron didn't haul people, as a rule, only goods. But a lot of other freighters didn't mind a companion if it meant a bit of extra money for their trouble.

He kept his voice as gentle as he could manage. "If you mean the driver, I'm afraid he didn't make it." He motioned toward the body in the grass.

As she took in the form, her pretty features twisted in horror. A noise came from her that sounded like a half-moan, half-grunt.

Then she slipped out of view.

Panic made him lurch forward. Had she stumbled? He couldn't remember how steep that slope was.

"Ma'am? Are you all right?" He hobbled as fast as he could manage, and the top of her head came into view again as he neared the rise.

She hadn't fallen but sat on the hillside.

He slowed his approach. She might need smelling salts or water. He was the last person who should be comforting a distraught female, but he couldn't very well climb back up in his wagon and ride away.

That new realization slowly webbed its way through his mind, wrapping around him like a noose rope. The driver was dead. The wagon damaged. The team run away.

This woman had no way to reach help unless Aaron took her there.

*Lord, what are You doing to me?* He squeezed his eyes shut for a heartbeat.

But he couldn't stand here bemoaning the reality. Best get on with things.

He forced himself to shuffle his weak leg forward, topping the rise and scrambling down the slope to where the woman sat. He removed his hat to address her, and she lifted red-rimmed eyes to him.

Only then did he realize that the mass of skirts around her bulged in the front. The dress she wore... It was the same style Mrs. Ingrid wore when she was about to give birth to little William.

His mouth went dry and his throat constricted. Not

only a woman, but one in the family way. He'd need to be extra gentle with her. It'd be ten days to Settler's Fort, Lord, help him. If they could make it that long, he'd deliver her safely into the hands of Doc Micah.

*Please, let us make it.*

He forced his gaze back up to her eyes, the ones that the hope had leaked out of. He knew that feeling. He'd lived the sadness.

He swallowed to bring enough moisture into his mouth to speak. "I'm Aaron Long." The words came out raspy, so he cleared his throat. "I assume you were riding on that wagon?" How had she gotten off before the wreck? Was she injured?

She nodded. "I had just climbed down. A wildcat jumped from a tree and landed on the mules." Her lips rolled in, her jaw trembling.

*Confound it. Help me here, Lord.*

The mules must have run for all they were worth to shake free of that cougar. Poor Driscoll.

He shifted farther down the slope so he didn't loom over her, then he softened his voice. "Are you hurt, ma'am?"

She shook her head, a dainty movement that didn't belong out here in these rough mountains. What was she doing in this land?

Was she really not injured? He slid a glance down the length of her, but those voluminous skirts covered everything. She would've said if she'd broken a limb, surely. She did climb the hill after all.

9

She hadn't spoken much, though, not since asking about the driver. Had shock altered her senses? "Can I get you something, ma'am? A drink of water?"

She locked those reddened eyes on him again, and the desperation in her expression gripped his chest. "What am I going to do?"

What indeed. He reached out a hand. "Come up the hill. I need to bring my rig over here, then we'll sort through what's best to do next."

She straightened, pulling her shoulders back and lifting her chin. Maybe regaining control of herself. But instead of taking his hand, she waved it away and turned on her hands and knees. Then she slowly worked up to a standing position. The task looked as if it required a great deal of effort, but with his own weakness, all he could do was grip her elbow and help her rise.

Her face formed a grimace as she straightened and placed both hands under her large belly, pulling her arm from his hold in the process. She squared her shoulders once more and started up the slope.

Obviously, she didn't want the likes of him touching her. Who could blame the lady?

As he followed, her every step looked as painful as his, and her breathing grew loud again. For his part, he had to lock his jaw against the burning in his foot where the flesh had rubbed raw.

At last they reached the flat ground at the summit, and she paused to suck in gulps of air. She still had her hands braced beneath her protruding middle, and the position outlined the expanse of the bulge there. That babe must be ready to come any time. Where was her husband?

She caught him looking, and heat surged up his neck. Before he could turn away, she offered a tight smile. "I have a month still. Long enough to reach Fort Benton."

Her gaze shifted toward the wagon and the still form nearby. "That's where Mr. Driscoll was taking me. He said there's a doctor there who can deliver my baby. Then when the ships start coming up the Missouri in the spring, we'll take the first one back to Philadelphia."

One month. *Lord, don't let that little one come early.*

"Is your husband waiting in Fort Benton for you?" If so, why hadn't he come for her instead of making her travel alone with a freighter? As this situation showed, travel in these mountains could be treacherous.

She lifted her chin, though she didn't look at him again. "He died on our homestead. My family lives back in Philadelphia."

Poor thing. She was having to navigate this challenging journey completely alone. And in her grief too. He'd have to take her with him to Settler's Fort then. And get her there as soon as he could manage so she'd have time to settle in before the baby came.

He followed her gaze to the wagon, bracing his hands at his waist as he studied the spilled contents. "It'll take me a couple hours to bury Driscoll. Then I have a little room on my load to add some of his." He shot a look her way. "Do you know which town he was hauling from so I can get the things back to their owners?"

Her brow lowered. "It was a small town with several mines. I might be able to remember the name if I think on it."

He nodded. He didn't cotton to the idea of taking part of the shipment without knowing whom to return it to, but if he left it here, others would scavenge with even less ability or desire to deliver the goods back to their owners. And he'd promised the Lord he'd do the right thing every chance he could.

He motioned toward the front of the wagon. "You can sit and rest while I get my team. I have water and a pot of beans I'm happy to share."

She eyed the spot, then headed that direction. He followed her, doing his best to keep his limp from being noticeable. As she sank onto one of the traces that stuck out about seat level, she seemed to wilt. Such a pretty thing, but exhaustion fanned lines away from her eyes.

He turned away, slapping his good leg to call Barney to his side. Not that the dog obeyed his commands very well. Aaron usually left him alone, but he didn't want the animal to stay and make this woman nervous.

He should have asked her name. They would have plenty of time for those niceties later, though. Ten long days on the bench beside her. Not the way he'd envisioned this last trip before winter.

He could endure it. God must have sent him to take her to safety at the time she needed it most. But was he the right man for the task?

He could only pray that the babe didn't come before they reached Doc Micah.

# CHAPTER 2

*N*ot only could Katie Barlow barely draw a full breath, but she desperately needed a chamber pot in this mountain wilderness. Hiding behind a large rock would have to do.

She eyed the retreating form of the man she'd found standing beside poor Mr. Driscoll. What an awful, horrendous event. Mr. Driscoll had reluctantly agreed to wait while she tended to business behind a rock down the slope, and she'd barely stepped from the wagon before the scream sounded. She could still hear the wildcat's cry as the beast leapt from a tree onto both mules' backs.

The animals brayed and leapt into a run, doing their best to shed the unwanted creature before it mangled their flesh. The hill hadn't slowed them down in the least, nor had Mr. Driscoll's shouts and urgent pulling on the reins.

And now... She allowed herself a glance over the wrecked wagon, and her gaze snagged on the white hair of that kind old man. A burn crept up to her nose and eyes, and she pulled her attention away. Was it her fault? If she hadn't asked to stop, would the wildcat have struck a moving wagon?

Though guilt burned within her, the personal matters she'd not yet tended to demanded attention. Again. Did all women go through this? At least the over-turned wagon offered a sizeable shield to protect her from view.

By the time the jingle of harness sounded in the distance, she'd stepped back around the conveyance and eyed the corner where goods spilled out. There was her carpet bag peeking from under the oilskin. That satchel she hated.

She could still remember the day Neil brought home the awful bag. His eyes brimmed with gusto for what he said had always been a secret dream. He'd gone and placed his business in the hands of its board of directors, announcing they would move to the Montana Territory. Some man he'd shared a luncheon with had planted the retched spark, not realizing how the raging fire would consume the staid man her parents once insisted she marry.

She'd tried to warn Neil that moving to this wilderness was preposterous. A hair-brained notion from too many greens and vinegar. He had no notion of the hard life out here. But he'd given her that look and squared his shoulders.

When he did that, she'd known there was no chance to convince him. Saying more would only set his decision firmer.

So she'd packed her clothing in a single trunk and loaded only the things that mattered most to her in that rose embroidered bag. Neil and the servants had overseen the packing of household goods since she'd had no idea what to take to a homestead in a valley so far away it wasn't even in the United States.

Neil promised this new life wouldn't be a toil for her, that she'd enjoy the adventure. The young couple he'd hired would handle the hard parts of keeping house in the wilderness—Lucy for the house and Sampson outdoors.

Of course, Neil hadn't counted on the pair slipping away in the night only a week after the completion of their cabin and barn. News of gold in Helena must have lured them.

Still, Katie had vowed to be a dutiful wife, so she learned to cook the animals Neil hunted and brought her freshly skinned. Not in her wildest imaginings had she thought her life would dissolve to such a disaster.

But she'd managed. She'd held her tongue and pressed back her tears.

And then the baby...and the tears refused to be restrained. How could she bring a new life into this loneliness? How could she love her child well while feeling so miserable?

It wasn't until she found Neil by the chopping block, his eyes lifeless and an ax still partially buried in his leg —too much blood spilling out, running in rivulets over the frozen ground around him—that she'd finally found the hope of leaving this place. Even now that image wrapped icy fingers around her throat.

This land was too much. She'd known it from that day when Neil laid the carpet bag at her feet, and now death had convinced her husband too.

This was her opportunity to leave. To return to a civilization where at least she knew the dangers. She could prepare herself for the hurtful remarks of women bent only on raising their own status among the fashionable set. For that matter, she could choose to stay home if she so desired, now that no insistent mother or success-minded husband squared his shoulders and commanded she play her role.

Now, at last, she could make her own choices.

All she had to do was get to Fort Benton and find the doctor Mr. Driscoll had promised resided there.

Dear Mr. Driscoll. She swallowed the fresh sting as her gaze slipped over to him. His kind face had made her believe God finally sent a nod her way.

And now this. Perhaps she'd been cursed to die in this land too.

The stranger limped up beside her and stopped a

few steps away. What had he said his name was? Aaron Tall? No. *Long.*

Aaron Long propped his hands at his waist and spoke in a grim voice. "I'll get started on a grave. Pull out anything that's yours from his wagon. And keep thinking about where Driscoll picked up this load from. I'd like to take on as much as we can carry and get it back to the owners once I drop you at Settler's Fort."

She jerked her head to better look at him. "Settler's Fort? Where is that? I need to get to Fort Benton." And not a day to waste.

The little one in her belly agreed with a flurry of activity that shot pain down Katie's leg. She fought to keep from showing the sharpness of it, yet she couldn't help but reach a hand to brace the spot where the babe had wiggled.

The man's gaze dropped to her middle, then jerked back up to her face. "That's where I've just come from, and it's a full two weeks' drive." His eyes lifted to the sky above them. "The weather's gonna turn bad soon, and I have to get this load to Settler's Fort."

Then his voice gentled as his gaze flicked to her belly again. "Mrs...." He paused, waiting for her to fill the next part.

"Barlow."

He nodded. "Mrs. Barlow, there's a good doctor there. He knows what he's doing." He patted the leg he'd been limping on. "He put this bone back together two years ago. Most would've cut it off, the inside was splintered so bad. But he didn't give up on me." He nodded toward her belly. "I'm sure he and Mrs. Ingrid both would be a great help. They have their own little one, a year and a half old now."

Her mind strained against the barrage of words, and she shook her head as he finished. "I have to get to Fort Benton. Is Settler's Fort on the way?" And would she believe him if he said yes? She couldn't backtrack. If she didn't make it to Fort Benton, how would she ever get back to Philadelphia in the spring?

She wouldn't be able to travel through this wilderness with a baby, not even if she could find a wagon to take her. Just look at what had happened to Mr. Driscoll. Only sheer luck had kept her from being on the seat with him when the wildcat struck. She could have ended up sprawled on the ground like that gentle man.

And her babe would have died with her. The thought sent shivers through her core. She had to protect her child.

Perhaps they'd be better off though.

She pushed aside the longing that tried to needle through. Sure, death would put an end to these endless challenges she faced at every turn. But she had control of her own destiny now, and she would make the life she wanted.

And to get there, she had to reach Fort Benton.

The man shook his head. "Settler's Fort is the opposite direction. About ten days' drive." Then his expression turned earnest. "I would take you to Benton if there were any way I could, but my load contains supplies urgently needed at Settler's Fort. If I'm delayed three and a half weeks, people will suffer. And we're likely to have quite a snowstorm between now and then. I might not make it back at all before spring."

Panic welled into her chest, nearly smothering the breath that was already so hard to take in with the weight of the baby pulling on her. "I have to get to Fort Benton. I'll wait for another wagon."

He didn't answer right away, just watched her, his brows lowered as though thinking hard. He wasn't as old as she'd assumed because of his limp. Maybe thirty years or so. His blue eyes weren't the kind of light, clear color that jumped out at you. They were almost navy, like a stormy night, hiding the depths of his thoughts.

Finally, he spoke again. "Sometimes, I go days on this road without passing another soul. Especially this late in the season. I can't leave you here without knowing for sure you have a safe ride. Plus there are wild animals lurking. That wildcat won't be hunting for a while since it had such a big meal, but there might be others."

His gaze flicked to her belly again. She didn't blame him. The babe was so big, it felt she carried a trunk in her midsection.

He shook his head, at first as though to clear his thoughts, but then the act became more deliberate. "Come to Settler's Fort now. I'll get you a place at the doctor's, then as soon as the snow thins enough to travel in the spring, I'll take you to Fort Benton." His expression eased like he was trying for something light-hearted. "You might even get there before the first steamboat."

She focused on breathing as she worked through that idea. All she really needed was a safe place to spend the winter, a doctor who could help with the birthing, and the ability to take the first steamer from Fort Benton once the Missouri thawed in the spring. If Aaron Long's words were correct, she might still have all that if she rode with him to Settler's Fort.

But could he be trusted to speak the truth? Men's promises had not held true in the past.

She ran her gaze over the nuances of his face. Pleasing features for sure. They didn't stand out as strikingly handsome, but as she took in each angle, the strength of his jaw and the clear symmetry of each line, the effect was enough to draw a person in.

But that wasn't what she searched for. The earnestness in his eyes did its best to soften her resolve, but he might have made an art of convincing innocents of his respectability for nefarious purposes.

She nearly snorted at that thought. She was no debutante. No man could look at her with desire, not in this condition. She would be a millstone around Mr. Long's neck, no matter how hard she tried not to be.

Still...she kept a hard glare on him. "Why would you want me to travel with you? Wouldn't it be much easier if you went your way and left me to worry about transportation on my own?"

He dipped his gaze to the ground, where the toe of his boot brushed the grass. "I can't leave you here. Neither my conscience nor my Lord would allow that." He looked up again. "Isn't there something I can do to ease your mind about Settler's Fort? It's a small mining town full of good people. My brother and I have lived there two years now, since they brought me in with my broken leg." He motioned again to the limb he didn't seem to put much weight on.

A bit of curiosity crept in, maybe so she wouldn't have to face the harder decision. But she gave way to it. "How were you injured? You said the bone broke into pieces?"

The lightness left his face, and his mouth formed a grim line. "Gun shot." He paused a moment. "I wasn't always a law-abiding citizen. I guess it's fair you know that before climbing on the bench beside me. My brother and I rode with a gang for about eleven years, stealing from people and businesses all through the Montana Territory. We were caught two years ago, and in that last shootout, a bullet went through my thigh bone. It was a miracle I didn't die like two of the other fellows.

My brother and I survived though. Nate had been wanting us to leave the group for years, and he set to work making restitution for our crimes as best he could. I was laid up in the doctor's clinic for over a twelve-month, but in truth, that turned out to be a good thing. The Lord needed that time to pull me out of the darkness I'd let myself sink into. Six months ago, I bought my wagon and team, and I've been freighting ever since."

He moved his hands back to his waist. "I'm determined to be the better man God's making me into, and you have my word I'll do everything I can to get you to Settler's Fort safe and sound. You'll have nothing to worry about from me."

The more he spoke—and revealed about himself—the more he shifted into a different person before her eyes. But it was one phrase that grabbed onto her throat and squeezed. *Needed that time to pull me out of the darkness.* That was exactly the way she'd felt since Neil brought her to that barren valley where there wasn't even a roof to sleep under. The darkness had been...smothering.

But now she'd finally clawed out, and maybe he'd done the same. They were...kindred spirits, in a way.

He still watched her, waiting for her answer. He wasn't pushing, not insisting she go where he told her to. He'd simply given her all the details and was letting her decide. Had anyone ever done that for her?

Before she could allow herself to second-guess the

decision, she nodded. "You bury him, and I'll pull what I need from the wagon."

She should offer to help with Mr. Driscoll, but laying Neil's bloodied body to rest still plagued her dreams. She couldn't bury another, not if there was someone else to do it.

Aaron Long had come just in time.

# CHAPTER 3

*a*aron couldn't summon the energy to re-hitch the mules, climb back on the bench, and ride another hour or two, then have to set up camp. In truth, it wasn't as much the energy he lacked as the fortitude to press forward amidst the throbbing in his foot.

Burying Driscoll had been hard on both body and heart. He'd not had a decent shovel to dig with, so he brought rocks to cover the man. And so much walking had rubbed the raw spots on his foot until the entire limb felt like he held it in the midst of a blazing fire. Mrs. Barlow had tried to help carry stones after a while, but he'd waved her off. He'd crawl with a rock strapped to his back before he'd allow a woman so near child-birth to hoist something that heavy.

Thankfully, the physical toil helped distract him from the melancholy of the task. Did Driscoll have family who would mourn him? How could Aaron let them know? There'd been no papers on his person to mention kin, so Aaron would need to search the wagon. Perhaps Mrs. Barlow would know.

Besides that, the man had died in the exact line of work Aaron performed. It could as easily have been him covered over with rocks, one by one.

Would he have wanted that? There was a time less than a year ago he would have welcomed leaving behind his miserable life. But God had changed him, had pulled him out of that miry pit. Given him purpose. Yet escaping this painful body meant meeting the Lord face-to-face. How could he not wish for that welcome event?

And so, with body and mind and heart exhausted, he motioned to a flat spot near the wagon still tipped on its side. "Let's camp here tonight. We'll start out first thing in the morning."

Mrs. Barlow straightened from folding a blanket and turned to him. "Camp here?" She lifted her gaze to the gray clouds covering the sky above them. "Shouldn't we go as far as we can before dark?"

In truth, she looked as weary as he felt, with the way her shoulders stooped. Tired lines fanned away from her eyes, far more than when he'd met her earlier.

He shook his head. "I think we both need rest. We'll start fresh tomorrow." He wouldn't normally have admitted his exhaustion, especially to a woman as pretty as she, but that bit of honesty might be the only thing that made her give in.

She shrugged and turned back to the blanket. "What should we do to make camp?"

Shouldn't she already know that? Surely she'd helped Driscoll set up and break down camp. Or perhaps the man hadn't allowed her to lift a hand because of her condition.

Aaron's pride might want to do the same, but his body wouldn't be able to manage it. At least not without scenes that would be far more injurious to his pride than simply allowing her to do a few of the easier tasks.

He turned toward where he'd tied the mules to graze. "I'm going to settle my team for the night. You'll find a pot of beans under the bench of my wagon and an oilcloth wrapped around blankets for bedding. There's dry kindling under there, too, and a tinderbox if you want to start the fire."

He had to lock his jaw to keep from groaning with every step as he hobbled to the grassy area where he'd tied Cain and Abel. He'd left their harness on because he'd assumed he'd be hitching them to the wagon again today, but now he could relieve them of the load and walk them down the slope to water.

What of Driscoll's team? Had the wildcat gotten the best of them? Two mules would be too large of a meal for one mountain lion, but the damages might have been deadly for them both, from the scene Mrs. Barlow had described. Whatever the cat didn't eat, wolves would surely be thankful for.

He gave Abel a pat on the neck. "I'll do my best to

keep you from that fate, boy. It's mostly in the Lord's hands though."

The mule shook its head and snorted, then rubbed its muzzle against Aaron's arm.

As much as he would've liked to accommodate his faithful friend, he pulled back so Abel's weight didn't knock him off balance. "Sorry, fellow. You can't push on my bad leg like that."

Doing everything required for the mules took nearly an hour, and he had to lean on Abel's shoulders like a walking stick to help him back up the hill. This mule was the older of the two brothers and definitely the steadier one, like his namesake. Cain possessed greater strength but a much more ornery spirit.

As they crested the rise to the level area where the wagon sat, he could nearly taste the beans he'd cooked the night before. Mrs. Barlow should have the fire going by now and the pot warmed. He'd be just in time to eat.

His gaze found the woman, perched in the spot where he'd pointed out to make camp. Where was the fire? She just sat there, legs sprawled out in front of her and arms propped behind. The position made the babe look even bigger than when she stood. She wasn't doing anything though, just watching his approach.

He led the mules toward her, and as he neared, he could see the blankets laid out into sleeping pallets. And there was the pot of beans and a few sticks of kindling, but still no fire.

He halted Cain and Abel in front of her. "Did you

not find the tinderbox?" He kept it in the same bundle as the blankets, so she couldn't have missed it.

"It's here." She nodded to the metal case tucked behind the sticks. "I'm not very good at starting a fire from a spark though."

So she hadn't even tried? The wood wasn't arranged to light, just stacked to the side. How could any person live to adulthood and not be able to start a fire from a tinderbox? Especially in this remote territory.

He held in his frustration and turned the team toward the spot he planned to tie them so they could graze in the night. "I'll be back to do it in a minute."

Once he settled the mules, Barney stepped from the woods to take up his place at Aaron's side. The dog trotted just out of reach as Aaron picked up firewood on his way toward the place where the woman still sat— doing nothing.

Even if she couldn't light the fire, she could have gathered more logs. Sure, she was likely tired, but did she not realize they'd need logs to burn for the night? Aaron had enough water in his flask to carry him to morning, but he sure hoped the woman had her own stash somewhere in Driscoll's wagon, for he might not be able to manage the hike down and back up that hill again. Had she thought of that?

As he reached her and dropped the logs with a thump, she sat up straighter. "Tell me what to do and I'll help."

He'd already done that, and she'd only accomplished half of what he asked. But he kept that gripe to himself. "We'll need several more loads of firewood. If it's too hard in your condition, I can get them." Perhaps the excitement of this day had been too much for her. Though if so, she shouldn't offer to help.

He settled onto the ground, and his body sagged with relief. His leg might not be willing to bear weight again tonight, so he could only hope she would be able to bring logs.

But as she lumbered onto her hands and knees, then her breaths turned heavy as she struggled to rise, regret pressed in on him. Carrying a child inside— growing a person—would surely be so much harder than putting up with the pain and challenges of his contrary leg.

From this sitting position, he couldn't do much to help her stand except grip her elbow and try to help push her up.

At last, she straightened and took in several deep breaths as she tucked one hand around her middle and straightened her skirts with the other. "That gets harder every day."

When she turned and waddled toward the trees, Barney gazed after her. The dog glanced back at Aaron, looking as if he wasn't sure who to stay with.

Aaron waved him on. "Go keep a watch on her."

The dog seemed to understand perfectly, for he trotted after the woman. Ever since the mutt had crept from the trees at the beginning of Aaron's second run from Settler's Fort to Fort Benton, the dog rarely left his side. He wouldn't come close enough to be touched, not even if Aaron held out savory meat or tried to creep up when the animal slept.

It seemed Barney had taken a liking to Mrs. Barlow. Perhaps that meant she was a decent sort, or maybe the dog sensed she needed a friend. Animals usually had keen intuition in both those areas. He suspected Barney had joined up with him all those months ago for the same reasons. Now, he must think this woman needed him more than Aaron.

The dog was probably right, but it didn't lessen the sting of rejection.

~

Katie pushed herself up to a sitting position in the darkness. The longer she laid here trying to force sleep, the more images batted about in her mind. Anytime the lifeless bodies of her husband or Mr. Driscoll tried to show themselves, she managed to push them away quickly enough.

But her thoughts simply wouldn't stop. Maybe walking around a while would help. Besides, she needed to use the tree cover for a moment of privacy. Perhaps she could bring back more firewood on her return.

Then maybe she could finally fall back to sleep.

She did her best not to make noise as she struggled

to standing. But when she glanced over at Mr. Long's sleeping form, the firelight reflected off his open eyes as he watched her.

"Do you need something?" He kept his voice low, though there was no one about save the dog, who'd already jumped to his feet.

She shook her head. "Sorry to wake you. I'm just going to the trees for a minute."

He nodded, adjusted his head, and closed his eyes. "Call out if you need me. I doubt the wildcat is still searching for a meal, but there might be other animals around. Barney will protect you."

She did her best not to shudder as she started for the woods. If she didn't need to go so badly, she wouldn't leave the light of the fire.

Hopefully she wouldn't have to call for Mr. Long. She'd been enough trial for him tonight. His eyes had revealed that truth when he came back from watering the mules.

He'd expected a meal warmed and ready for him. Just like Neil had every night when he came in from work. And just like she'd done with Neil so many times, she'd disappointed Mr. Long.

Why couldn't she manage something as simple as starting a fire with flint and steel? It seemed every other person in this land could do so.

She'd tried to learn. So many times, she'd tried.

Back in Philadelphia, the servants kept the fires burning, so she'd been able to easily light a candle or lantern from the hearth. Lucy had seen to fires in the cabin at first. It wasn't until those two ran off that she'd been faced with this apparent deficit of skill. Neil had tried to teach her, but they both finally gave in to the fact that she was inept. From that day on, she'd done her best to never allow the coals in their hearth to die.

For the two days she'd ridden with Mr. Driscoll, he'd handled the fire-making, so she'd never had to reveal her inability.

But she'd not been able to hide it from Mr. Long. She would surely disappoint him in other ways during their time together—she likely had already this evening. If not before, waking him when she rose must have been frustrating. Neil had hated to be pulled from sleep in the night.

She only had ten days with this man, though, then he'd be shed of her. She had sufficient funds to pay for lodging in Settler's Fort for the winter. Mr. Long wouldn't have to see her again.

After attending to matters, she searched for logs she could manage. The dog stayed close as she moved about, yet never near enough for her to pet him. "Are you hungry, fella?" Maybe a bit of food when they were back at camp would encourage him. She still had smoked meat from Mr. Driscoll's pack.

She crept back to the fire as quietly as she could manage, but even though she laid each log gently on the stack, they shifted and clattered as they settled. She had to work to catch her breath as she straightened.

This baby pulled so heavily on her shoulders, her lungs barely had room to draw a deep breath.

She'd surely awakened Mr. Long again, but he lay with his eyes closed. She moved to kneel beside the crate of foodstuffs and other necessities she'd pulled from Mr. Driscoll's wagon and riffled around inside until she found the pouch of meat.

The dog sat about three armlengths away, watching her.

She eased down to a sitting position to make herself more comfortable. This could take patience. After breaking off a piece, she tossed it midway between her and the animal. He studied the scrap, then eyed her. At last, he seemed to decide accepting the bribe wouldn't endanger him. He crept forward, took the meat in his jaw, then eased back to his original spot.

Good. He clearly didn't plan to make this easy, but at least he was susceptible to the treat.

The next bite, she dropped a little closer, only an armlength away from herself. He didn't hesitate as long this time but moved in and took the meat, then retreated—not as far away.

Only the fact that Mr. Long was trying to sleep kept her from talking to the dog, but silence might be best. She hadn't been around long enough for her voice to reassure him.

After dropping a third piece closer to herself, she kept her hand outstretched partway while he came forward to take it.

She made the fourth bite long enough that she could grip the end and hold it out to him. As it hovered just above the ground, the dog eyed the situation carefully.

*Come on, boy. You can trust me.*

She kept herself as still as she could manage, though her arm began to tremble. Why did her entire body feel so weak these days?

At last, the mutt crept forward, gingerly took the piece, then dropped to its belly to gnaw on it.

Ever so slowly, she pulled her hand back as she smiled. The first time she'd smiled in months. He'd not even walked away to eat the meat. She'd been hoping for a chance to pet the animal, but this seemed such a victory, such a show of trust, she had no need to press for more.

If only she could succeed so well in the rest of her life. But the obstacles that constantly rose up to thwart her were far less pleasant than a skittish dog.

As she crawled back to her blankets, her mind began to conjure what might arise tomorrow. She forced the thoughts away. She'd never get to sleep if she allowed her free rein in that direction.

After pulling the blankets around her, she stared into the fire, then through the flames to the man lying on the other side. She was placing her life in his hands.

So far, he'd not given her cause for concern, but they'd only spent a few hours together. What might happen over the course of ten days?

Whatever came, she would have to face it. She was alone in this journey, able to make up her own mind as she'd always wanted to.

If only the freedom didn't come with so much risk of failure.

# CHAPTER 4

*A*aron eyed the woman on the bench beside him. She kept shifting around, sometimes straightening and gripping her belly, other times rubbing her back. She'd done those things yesterday after he'd found her at the wrecked wagon, but not as often as today.

Had he pushed her too hard? In truth, he'd been delaying stopping for the night because his foot ached so much, he wasn't altogether sure he could walk on it. The blisters must be festering.

But he'd be a cad if he let his own aches cause her trouble from too much time bouncing on this hard bench as the wagon maneuvered rocks and ruts in the trail.

He sent another glance her way. "Are you ready to stop for the night?"

"Any time you are." Her voice came out tight. He should've stopped an hour ago.

He reined the team to the edge of the road, then pulled back on the leathers. "Whoa, Cain. Whoa, Abel."

The mules obliged, Abel dropping his head as he breathed out a long sigh. Cain bobbed his nose, chewing at the bit.

Aaron set the brake, then motioned to the area between the wagon and the cliff that rose up beside them. "There's a good spot to camp out of the wind."

She nodded but didn't move to dismount. He should hurry down and around the wagon to help her. But the thought of hurrying anywhere made him want to say a word he'd not spoken in many months. *Help me, Lord.*

He reached for the wooden bar to give him extra support as he dismounted. "Stay put. I'll come help you."

"I can do it."

His offer seemed to be the push she needed to disembark on her side, and she managed the feat quicker than he.

But as he was still gripping the bar for balance, he could see the way she clutched her belly and slowly straightened. They were a pair, the two of them.

He released the wagon and hobbled to unfasten the traces. "I'm going to water the mules and settle them for the night. Stretch your legs if you like. I'll help with camp when I get back." He'd have better expectations for tonight.

The dog followed along beside the team, a surprise since he'd appeared to desert to the woman the night before. But maybe it wasn't a contest. Barney could wander wherever he wanted, and Aaron could hardly blame him for being charmed by the kindness of that pretty lady. Maybe he joined him now for a drink of water.

Every step made Aaron's foot burn with the rubbing of the blisters, and he leaned heavily on Abel's shoulders as they approached the creek. At last, he got the animals hobbled where they could graze through the night, but he could no longer conceal the severity of his limp as he trudged back to camp.

Mrs. Barlow looked up from the crate she rummaged through as he approached. The way her gaze honed on his leg showed she didn't miss the change in his gait. Hopefully she wouldn't say anything though.

She'd laid out the fire but hadn't kindled it yet. It looked like she had the makings of a meal ready also— a kettle and twin plates prepared with the cornbread he'd fried up last night. Hopefully she planned to add meat to that meal. If not, he had jerky he could pull out.

Once he'd lowered himself, his leg burned with relief. He clenched his jaw to keep from groaning while his body adjusted. The pain in his foot seared all the way up to his knee now. He'd have to pull the boot off and see what he could do about those blisters.

But first... He reached for the tinderbox. "Would you

like me to teach you how to start a fire?" He tried to keep his tone casual, as though it didn't matter whether she said yes or no. In truth, if she didn't learn this skill soon, she'd never survive in these western territories.

Her regard tickled the fine hairs on his neck, but he didn't look her way. When she spoke, her voice sounded hesitant. "Others have tried to teach me before."

That wasn't quite a no, so maybe he could just talk through his actions. He opened up the tin box. "Not sure if you tried it with charcloth or not, but that makes all the difference for me. Once I have my twine opened up, I just hold the cloth against the flint like this"—he placed the tiny strip of fabric near the edge of the flint where it would catch a spark—"then I strike the steel against the flint. When I get a good spark on the cloth, I blow it a little." He blew a thin stream of air across the spark, then another until the cloth glowed red.

"Now I can place it against the twine threads and wrap them around it like so." He blew another bit of air into the bundle, and the flame leapt to life.

He placed the burning twine in the middle of the kindling Mrs. Barlow had laid in a pile. "You've readied things well. I'm just going to tuck this under the smallest sticks and stand them up over it like an Indian lodge." He sent a glance her way. "Have you ever seen a teepee?"

She was studying his hands with an intense expression as he shifted the twigs around so they'd have the best chance of catching fire. "No, but a man who stopped by our homestead told of living in one when he stayed a winter with the Crow." She spoke the words distractedly, her gaze never straying from his task.

The flame was already licking up the dry twigs, so he moved larger pieces to form a layer around the smaller ones. "I try to always have the driest wood when I'm starting a fire. Later on, we can use fresher logs, but we need wood that will catch easily right now."

She nodded. With the way she hung on every movement, surely she would be able to do this herself. "Tomorrow night, I'll let you strike the flint."

When he glanced her way again, she'd finally moved her gaze from his hands up to his eyes. She looked a bit like a wary horse, not sure if she could trust him not to hurt her. He'd probably pushed far enough for this evening.

He nodded toward the kettle. "We won't have good coals for a while, but you can bring that in next to the flame if you want to start the water heating."

She did as he said. "I've some salted ham to go with our meal. And I have some tea left in my box. A quarter hour should see it ready."

Tea. He'd not tasted any since he last sat at Mrs. Ingrid's table. Normally, he made do with water or coffee in the mornings, but as the notion settled in his mind, the idea of something warm with a rich flavor sounded good about now.

A quarter hour would give him enough time to walk

back to the creek and remove his boot to look at the blisters. They could probably use a washing.

"That sounds like a hearty meal. In the meantime, I'll refill our water pouches." Rising to his feet in front of anyone could sometimes lay his pride low, the way he had to struggle for balance with his weak limb. But in front of this woman, what he wouldn't do to be able to push up to standing like any normal man. Once more, he had to grit his teeth to keep from grunting as his shoe leather rubbed the raw places in his flesh.

As before, Mrs. Barlow watched his face far too carefully. He turned away and started toward the water, barely remembering to grab the pouches before he limped away.

At the creek, his body crumpled to the ground now that he didn't have a beautiful lady scrutinizing his movements. He filled the pouches first since he'd likely muddy the water with his foot. Once he'd loosened the laces on his boot, he had to work to get the shoe off. It felt like the leather had shrunk.

Through the three holes in his stockings, angry flesh glared up at him. As he tried to remove the woolen material, the fabric stuck to his feet where the blood had dried. Or perhaps that was liquid from the putrid festering. He peeled the layers off, finally freeing his foot from the confines of the wool.

The bare limb looked worse than he'd expected. The whole foot had swollen, and large patches of red skin surrounded the oozing blisters.

He lowered the foot into the water, his entire body clenching against the mixture of frigid water and searing pain. Finally, his body eased enough that he could draw breath, and the longer he kept the limb in the creek, the more numb the skin became. If only he could sit here all night. If he attempted it, he may lose the toes to frostbite, for the weather had already begun to dip close to freezing.

He tried to gauge ten minutes, then pulled the foot out of the water. He could no longer feel any burning in the flesh, but the swelling hadn't gone down, and what little of the skin that wasn't red before now glared brightly from the cold.

The stocking had become a pitiful object, riddled with holes and stiff with dried blood and pus. It needed a good washing and mending, but he had nothing else to put on, and his feet would grow even worse in the boot with no stocking at all. The best he could settle for was turning it around so the holes that had been on top of his foot now exposed the bottom. This would likely result in blisters underneath his foot and more holes in the stocking where the boot rubbed on top. Maybe he could find cloth to wrap his foot in before then.

But when he tried to pull his boot on over the swollen appendage, the swelling had grown far too large to tuck inside the leather. The effort reignited the flame in his foot, and the more he tugged, the more he wanted to either swear or cry. This was ridiculous. Would he have to now trudge back with only a stocking on this foot? At least it wouldn't make his limp any worse than it had already become. Not having the leather rub would feel better. Should he remove the other shoe too? Mrs. Barlow would surely think him a daft invalid. Certainly not a man to be admired.

He'd come to terms with the fact that no woman would consider him a catch with this weak leg. But spending so much time with a lady like Mrs. Barlow... Well, that made a man wish for better.

Made him wish *he* were better.

~

*W*as the drop in temperature the cause of Mr. Long's pain? Katie studied him as he limped back to their camp. Maybe she shouldn't be so obvious in watching, but she had neither the strength nor desire to cater to polite manners. And this man needed help.

That was why she was brewing willow bark tea for his pain. Was something else wrong, though? The limp was a great more severe than yesterday. Had he hurt himself since then?

As he neared the camp, she caught sight of his stockinged foot. He *must* have injured himself. Either that or the shoe made his leg hurt worse.

Just watching the way he eased himself down a tiny bit at a time made her own body hurt. He exhaled a long breath once he settled, but he didn't look her way.

He also tucked his foot where his trousers mostly covered it, so she couldn't get a good view of the stocking. She might have to directly ask him what had happened.

First, though, she handed him the plate she'd prepared. Men always responded better with a full belly.

He took the food with a "Thanks," and then she poured tea from the kettle.

"This will taste better after it brews longer, but here's a cup to start with." The willow bark would be bitter. Too bad she didn't have sugar or molasses to sweeten it with.

"Aren't you going to eat?"

He hadn't taken a bite yet but motioned toward her own plate, which she hadn't touched.

"I'll get to it. Here's your tea." In truth, her body was almost too weary to eat. She would do what she needed to help Mr. Long before collapsing onto her blanket. The pains around her belly had come more frequently this afternoon. Nothing so strong she couldn't stand it, and not steady like her housewifery book said to watch for. Just exhausting.

He took the cup and sipped, but his brow stayed lowered. He seemed to be contemplating something. "Aren't you feeling well?"

Now it was her turn not to meet his gaze. "Just tired." She adjusted the kettle back among the logs on the fire.

"Lie down then. I can do what's left to be done."

She looked over at his foot, where only a snippet of gray wool showed. "Are you hurt? A new injury, I mean?" She couldn't stretch out for the night until she'd done everything she could for him.

He shifted, covering the foot a little more. "Just a rub from my boot. Nothing much."

She met his gaze. "I have a salve that should keep any blisters from festering. Is there a hole in your stocking? I don't have darning needles, but I might be able to patch it."

He shook his head a little too quickly. "I'd use a salve if you have it. No need to concern yourself about the holes."

More than one hole then. And since he seemed so skittish about the whole situation, his blisters had likely already festered. That must be adding to his limp. She had a feeling this man didn't like to show pain.

She searched her carpet bag for the cream Sarah had taught her to mix. She had an extra pair of wool stockings too. Would he accept them if she offered? They were a simple cream color, no fancy embroidery or ruffles. And the weave was loose enough that the pair would likely stretch to fit his feet. If he was in the condition she suspected, his own stocking would do little to help and he might be willing—or rather, desperate enough—to use hers.

She pulled out the salve and the garments and handed them to him, then kept her voice casual enough to ease his pride. "If you've a hole in yours, put these on to keep the boot from rubbing more. You wouldn't want the blisters to fester and burn. When they reach that state, the foot will often swell, and sometimes the fever will overtake the rest of your body. You'd be laid low in only a day or two. And I need to get to that town and its doctor." She could only hope the description of what was to come, maybe some of which he was already experiencing, would encourage him to care for the wounds properly.

He took the jar and stockings, but his gaze had sharpened on her. "Do you think the babe will come early?"

She didn't have the strength to ease his fears too much, but she could offer a simple fact. "I'm supposed to have several weeks still. Maybe as much as a month."

Though that didn't ensure this little one would wait the full length of time. The housewifery book made that clear.

For now, she needed to allow him a moment alone to care for his foot. She shifted to her knees so she could work up to standing. "I'm going to the water for a minute."

And when she came back, she would ignore the call of the blankets no longer.

# CHAPTER 5

*T*he salve had worked a miracle.

Aaron stared at his foot as he sat on the creek's bank in the early morning light. Raised red patches still outlined the open sores, but the foot was no longer swollen. The tightness had left his skin, though the flesh still burned.

Not as fiery as the night before, even when he'd walked on the limb. Whatever was in that salve, he needed to get his own tin of it. The container wasn't labeled, so he'd have to ask the name so he could order it in the spring. Could he wait that long? Maybe she had an extra container he could purchase from her.

After applying a fresh dose and pulling on the stocking she'd given him, he eased his foot into the boot. The fit was tight, but at least he could manage it now.

After working himself to his feet, he scooped up the

full kettle and his own clean but hole-ridden stocking and started back toward camp. Barney trotted nearby, out of reach as usual.

When he reached their fire, tucked back behind the wagon, Mrs. Barlow sat upright on her pallet, blankets pulled around her. Her hair was mussed, and her eyes squinted as though she'd just awakened, or maybe hadn't yet fully reached that state. Her face looked a little puffy too. Was that normal for her when awakening, or perhaps it had to do with her condition?

She studied him as he approached. "Is your foot improved?"

"It is." He reached for two more logs to add to the fire. "That salve you gave seems to be working better than I'd expected. Can you tell me where you ordered it? And mayhap I could buy this tin from you?"

"You can have it. I make the cream from several different barks and roots that are known for their healing properties." She sucked in a breath between gritted teeth and straightened, her hand moving to her back.

His own belly clenched. "Is something wrong?" Surely this wasn't her time. She had a month left.

But maybe something else was paining her.

She shook her head. "Just the baby moving a lot this morning. That's why I didn't get much sleep."

No wonder she looked so weary.

"Would you like coffee or tea? I can cook up corn

mush too. Something warm might make you and the baby both happy."

She looked hesitant. "Maybe tea. Thank you."

He eased himself to the ground and started the water heating as he prepared the pot for the tea. Mrs. Barlow lay back on her bed pallet, looking like she didn't have the strength to stay upright. He tried not to stare, but her face had lost most of its color. Would she be well enough to travel today?

Sitting up on the bench for so many long hours at a time was hard on anyone, but it was too much to ask a woman so near her term, especially as weary as she looked now. He could move the load around a little, maybe strap a few crates beside him on the bench, and make a little bed for her in the back. That way she could rest or sit up as she wanted.

When the mush and tea were ready, she still lay in her blankets. He brought a cup and bowl over to her, and she pushed her covers aside. "I'm sorry. I should have prepared the food. You don't have to serve me." As she sat up, her face pinched in tight lines.

"It's the least I could do after how you helped me last night. I didn't realize you made the salve. Do you have training as an apothecary?"

Her face brightened a tiny bit. "No, but when I was a girl, our housekeeper knew a great deal about herbal remedies. She taught me, then gave me some of her books that identify plants and which parts are good for healing."

Though the weariness marking her features didn't fade, her eyes and voice lit as she spoke.

"You've proven yourself an apt student."

As she took a sip of tea, her body jerked a little. Her hand moved to her belly, and her lips pressed together.

His own gut tightened. "Is the baby moving again?"

She gave a single nod, then she breathed out a slow exhale. "I suppose she's ready to come out."

Panic surged up his throat. "Not for a month yet, right?"

She gave a tight smile. "I hope so."

She *hoped* so? He had to get her to Settler's Fort. "What can I do to help? I'll make a bed in the back of the wagon. You'll be more comfortable there."

Her smile held relief. "Thank you."

He moved back to the pot and kettle. "I'll scarf down some food, then go hitch the team. We can head out as soon as you're ready."

~

She couldn't go on much longer.

Katie gripped the crate handle she'd been clutching all day, curling into herself as the burning pain wrapped around her belly. She would have to ask Mr. Long to stop.

The pains were taking her breath and all her concentration to endure, and each bump and jolt of the wagon felt like a red hot knife searing her flesh.

She had no notion of where they were, only that four days had passed since she left the homestead and they'd been climbing upward ever since they stopped to let the horses rest at noon.

As that pain ebbed, she uncurled herself and lifted her head to call up to the bench. "Mr. Long?" Her voice came out weak and shaky.

"Yes, ma'am?" He twisted to look at her. "What's wrong?"

She hated to show her weakness, but she had to. "Do you plan to make camp soon?" He must think her a weakling, getting to lie here all day and still asking to stop early. These pains were real, though. Her time had come. She would have to tell him that at some point, but that could wait a little longer.

"I see an overhang up ahead, and I think that's a water flow near it. About five more minutes all right?"

Her body sagged with relief. "That's good."

As he called encouragement to the mules, another pain gripped her middle, enfolding her with the burning pressure that made it hard to breathe. She struggled to take in slow, steady breaths as the house-wifery book had said. As soon as they made camp, she would pull it out, though she'd memorized the entire section about what to expect during childbirth. Could she manage everything alone?

The fear she'd been forcing aside all day pressed in. How could she possibly give birth to a babe without help? She would have to ask Aaron for things she couldn't do herself. Would he be squeamish? Maybe he'd refuse altogether.

*God, if You've ever cared about me, please, help me now.*

That pain released, and thankfully, another one hadn't yet begun by the time Mr. Long reined in the mules. She had to get out of the wagon before another round came on. If it caught her in the middle of climbing out, things would be so much worse.

With one hand under her belly for support, she pushed herself upright, then reached for the side to climb over.

"I'll come back and help you." Mr. Long's voice nudged into her awareness, but she didn't let it slow her.

She had to get out of this wagon, and she couldn't wait on him.

He reached her as she lifted her second leg over the side, and his grip on her arm did help steady her.

"Easy now." The gentle murmur of his voice settled her insides even more. Did he suspect she'd reached her time?

Another pain wrapped around her, wiping away that thought and all others. She gripped the wagon and focused on pulling in a deep breath, then blowing it out in a slow stream. Another breath in, then out.

Mr. Long's grip left her arm, and his voice murmured in the background, but nothing penetrated her focus on breathing. She wanted to claw away from this pain, but she couldn't draw enough air to do anything but tremble.

At last, the agony subsided. She kept gripping the wagon, gathering strength to stand upright. Her thighs still shook, barely able to hold her even with help.

Again, the soothing timbre of Mr. Long's voice sounded at her side. "I laid out your blankets if you think you can move to them."

The thought of a soft place to collapse infused a bit of strength, especially a bed that didn't bounce and jolt with every breath. She eased upright and removed one hand from the wagon to make sure her legs could support her.

She didn't wilt, so she turned toward the blankets he'd laid out. She didn't have the courage to meet his gaze, but he took her arm. The extra balance helped. His other hand rested on her back.

The touch felt a little like the offering of support. Maybe he would be willing to help when she needed him in the coming ordeal. Or maybe he would prove squeamish.

Either way, they would find out soon.

# CHAPTER 6

*God, you have to fix this. I have no idea what to do.*

Aaron turned away from the woman he'd just helped to her blankets and scrubbed his hands through his hair as he stared at the wagon. What should he do first? Unhitch the team and get them settled so he could focus on Mrs. Barlow? She might need her belongings first. And food. And water.

He had a feeling this was her time, though there was still a chance she was simply ill. She'd not answered his questions about what bothered her.

He pulled everything he could think of she might need from the wagon and laid it near enough she could reach the bags and crates. Then he bent down near her head. "What can I do to help you?"

She lay still with her eyes closed, curled on her side. She didn't open them as she spoke. "Nothing right now."

"I need to unhitch the mules. Would you rather I stay close for a while?"

Her eyes, when she opened them, held a glassy look. "I can handle it myself for a while. But when the baby comes, I'll need your help."

It must be her time. He swallowed, then took in a long deep breath and eased it out. "I'll do whatever you ask. Let me get Cain and Abel settled, then I'll be with you as long as you need me."

As he unfastened the straps connecting the team to the wagon, his mind swirled around what he might have to do. In truth, he had no notion what he might be needed for. He'd never been around for a birthing, had barely even known a woman's company growing up. Not after his parents died when he and Nate were eight.

After those awful weeks the two of them survived on their own, they'd lived a year with Aunt Bertie and Uncle Ronald. But then they'd been passed to Paul and spent the next four years helping to build up his farm. Those were the years he remembered most, and there hadn't been a female in sight. When Paul finally married, they'd all come west to the Montana territory. Unfortunately, smallpox had claimed Paul and his new bride, leaving Aaron and Nate once again alone.

So no, he knew nothing about the birthing process, not even in dogs or horses. But she'd spoken those words—*I'll need your help*—and they'd clutched somewhere deep in his soul. His twin brother was the only one who'd ever needed Aaron, but Nate had Laura now.

After their wedding, Aaron hadn't expected to be needed ever again.

When he returned to Mrs. Barlow, she had her chin tucked into her chest, her breathing slow and labored.

"How can I help you?"

She didn't answer, just kept those slow, hard inhales and releases. At last, the tightness in her seemed to ease. She opened her eyes and turned a weary expression to him. "We'll need blankets. And hot water. A fire."

Those he could do. After he'd gathered enough kindling and wood to light a blaze, he settled himself to accomplish the task. Mrs. Barlow lay on her blanket, staring in his direction with that glassy gaze. Maybe this would be a good time to ask questions.

Best to start with the most important. "Do you, um, know how the birthing should go?"

Her gaze sharpened on him. "I have a book in my carpet bag. *The Tennessee Housewifery*. There's a chapter on what to expect in childbirth."

That was a start at least. He could pull out the manual and see if it offered anything helpful. "Have you seen a birthing?"

"Not me, but our housekeeper, Sarah, helped a midwife sometimes. She told me what she did when things didn't go well."

He eyed her. "Sarah. She's the one who taught you how to make the salve?"

She nodded, and her expression softened a little.

"She sounds like a special lady. Talented." And important to this woman.

With a groan, she gripped the edge of the blanket and curled in. "Here's another."

She twisted that flimsy fabric as her face went pale and the tendons on her neck stood out. He knew pain like that, but to watch her endure it...his insides squeezed. That blanket wouldn't help her fight against the agony. She needed something sturdier.

He pulled a thin branch from the stack and moved over to her side. "Grip this. It'll help."

Her hands snatched the stick, nearly jerking it from him as a guttural groan tore from her. Tears leaked from her eyes, running over the bridge of her nose to disappear into the shadows.

His own body ached, pressing in his chest and crawling through every part of him. She was enduring this pain so quietly, far different from what he'd done back in the worst of his dark days.

Finally, the whiteness of her fingers faded to normal color, and her face began to relax. Her breathing lost its coarse straining but stayed deep, as though the air could finally find its way inside and her body craved more.

The hair around her face had pulled from her braid and lay matted across her cheek. He reached to brush it back, but caught himself just before his fingers touched her skin. Maybe she wouldn't appreciate such an intimate action. But he had a feeling they were about to become even more familiar than this, and his job here was to do whatever he could to help during the ordeal.

So he shifted the hair aside, his coarse stubby fingers probably scratching her delicate skin. As he stroked the soft locks into place, the velvety feel of the strands nearly made him weave his fingers deeper. Did every woman's hair feel so rich?

She opened her eyes, jerking him from the thought. He pulled his hand back and cleared his throat as he scrambled for something to say. "Do you want some water? Or should I make you tea?"

She opened her mouth, drawing his attention to her parched lips. "Water." Her voice rasped. The drink would help her throat, and he had some grease saved that would soften the chapping of her lips.

When he brought the cup, she raised up on an elbow to take it. Then he opened the tin of grease and handed it over. "This will help your lips."

After drinking half the cupful, she sank back to the blankets and handed the mug to him, taking the grease.

Hopefully she wouldn't mind another question or two. "Do you know, um, about how much time you have left? I mean, how long until the baby...?"

She rubbed the grease over her mouth. "I don't know. Sometime in the night, I think." Her gaze glanced to his, then away again. "I don't really...I mean, I think it's hard to say for sure."

He nodded. "I imagine so." But he didn't miss the uncertainty in her expression.

How afraid she must be, having to endure this experience on the side of a mountain, in the elements, and with no doctor less than a week's ride away. With only the knowledge from a chapter in a housewifery book and a few stories told her as a child.

And with *him* her only help.

Well, he'd do everything in his power to aid, and he'd give as much encouragement as he could. And he'd arm himself with knowledge. "Do you mind if I read that chapter you mentioned?"

A bit of color slipped into her cheeks, but she pointed to her carpet bag. "It shouldn't be hard to find in there."

He reached for the case, and thankfully, as soon as he unfastened the latch, the book's spine stared up at him.

As he returned the bag to its place, a groan from behind made him spin around. Mrs. Barlow's eyes squeezed tight again, and her grip on the stick whitened once more.

*Lord, give her strength. Show me what I can do to help. And let this babe come quickly.*

He moved back to her side and settled in with *The Tennessee Housewifery*. He had a lot of studying to do.

*T*he book must be wrong.

Either that or the author had been afraid to go into the true detail of what a woman would endure in this awful process.

Aaron's entire body clenched as Mrs. Barlow released a guttural howl, a sound that began deep in her belly where the pain must be unendurable. She knelt on hands and knees as she fought the intensity of whatever agony clenched her. In the firelight, the back of her skirt showed a darker blue from whatever wetness had leaked out all over her several hours ago.

It couldn't be easier to endure the pain on her hands and knees, though she might be trying to crawl away from whatever clawed inside her.

As soon as this round eased, he spoke. "Why don't you come back to the blankets? Surely that will be more comfortable."

She only groaned, this time a quieter sound, yet from just as deep a place. Then she lowered her head to the ground, coming down onto her elbows. "There's nowhere comfortable. When will this end?"

He'd been begging God to answer that same question for hours now. "Surely you're close. Do you want more water?" It was such a flimsy offering, yet he could think of nothing else to bring any sort of relief.

She didn't answer, just stayed in that position with her head on the ground and her rear in the air.

Surely there was something he could say to distract

her from her misery. Maybe get her thinking about the reward for all this hard work. "Mrs. Barlow, I—"

"Don't call me that." Her voice came out soft, almost mellow. But the words were anything but relaxed. "My name is Katie."

What did she mean? Had she not been married? Or was Barlow not her surname? Or maybe she couldn't stand to think of her past at a time like this. Her deceased husband who should be here with her now.

No matter the reason, this was a request he could easily oblige. "All right, Katie. Call me Aaron." It did seem like they could use Christian names at this point. "I was going to ask if you'd picked out a name for the baby."

She was quiet for a moment, and her voice came out in that same soft tone. "I thought maybe Sarah Rebecca."

Sarah after the woman who'd meant so much to her. "Is Rebecca...?"

"My mother's name."

"Ahh." He'd wondered about her parents, but she hadn't spoken of them. That might be a question for later though. "So you think the babe will be a girl?"

She turned her face toward him, though she kept her head pressed to the grass. The firelight flickered in her eyes. "I don't know. I just haven't been able to come up with any boy names I like."

Did he dare ask the obvious? His mouth formed the

words before his mind could decide. "What about its father?"

Her face was impossible to read with all its shadows. "I suppose he could carry Neil's name." She turned toward the ground again. "Neil would have liked that." Her voice didn't seem to hold any softness or sentiment. Had she locked those feelings away in her grief? Or had theirs not been a marriage of love? Perhaps convenience.

He couldn't remember the last time he'd wanted to know a person's story as much as he did this woman's. Now wasn't the time to ask.

She let out another groan and inched her knees forward, tucking them under herself. She straightened her arms in front of her, lifting her shoulders up like a cat stretching. Yet the tension radiating from her held not a shred of relaxation. He moved to her side, but what could he do? The book had said that to calm a laboring woman, he could rub her back or wipe her face with a damp cloth. Katie wasn't hysterical like the guide had said some women became, but maybe she would appreciate some of those same touches.

He reached out to rub her back, but his hand faltered midair. He forced himself to finish what he began, resting his fingertips on the back of her dress. She was a mixture of softness and tension, and he made his hand move upward toward her neck, then around and down to form a full circle on her upper back. Had he ever touched a woman like this? Not since his mother, he was nearly certain.

His chest ached from not drawing in a full breath, so he forced his body to relax as he continued the motion. No matter how strange or uncomfortable this felt, if it helped her even a little, he would do it.

Her warmth seeped into his cold hand, easing up his arm and relaxing his muscles. Katie's body seemed to tense even more, if that were possible.

"Oh, oh, oh. No." She groaned, or maybe moaned, the words, their agony seeping from her deepest parts. "I can't. I can't."

He moved his other hand to join with the first, stroking his thumbs up her back to her shoulders. "You can. You're doing remarkably. You can do this."

She whimpered, and her breaths came in quick bursts.

*Lord, help her. Please!*

This round of pain seemed to last an hour, but finally subsided, her body easing one breath at a time. She sank to the ground, face down with her arms outstretched and her knees curled up underneath her.

He continued to work his hands over her back, at times rubbing a large circle, then using his thumbs to stroke out the knots around her shoulders.

Did she want him to stop? Perhaps she couldn't rest with him moving around so.

He slowed his hands until they rested motionless on her back.

"Don't stop." Her voice barely held enough strength to reach him.

With that question answered, he resumed the movement. "Tell me if I'm doing something that hurts."

"It all hurts." She groaned the words, then her body tensed again. Another pain must be coming on.

She pushed up, nearly knocking his hands aside as she rose on all fours. "I think she's coming. It's..." The words faded in a growl as she curled her back and half-groaned, half-howled a throaty cry.

His heart leapt into his throat. *God, what do I do?* The book had said the head would come first—crowning, they called it. The babe couldn't come with her up on her knees like that. It would fall to the ground, and who knew how badly that would injure such a fragile body.

"Katie, can you lie down? The baby."

With another groan, not as loud this time, she collapsed onto her side, panting for breath. Had this pain subsided? It didn't seem as long as the other recent ones, though maybe harder.

"You have to check." She struggled for air. "If you see...the baby."

*No.* As much as he'd been trying to prepare himself for this. He couldn't do it.

She must have sensed his hesitation, for her eyes opened and she glared at him. "Aaron, I need to know if the baby's coming out."

He swallowed, forcing moisture into his throat. *Lord, give me strength. Help me do this for her. And for You.*

# CHAPTER 7

*H*e'd never seen such a perfect, fragile—
and yes, strange looking—baby. Aaron
could only stare at the wriggling body in his hands.

"Is it alive? A boy or girl?"

Katie's frantic questions pulled him from his stupor,
and he sent a look down the length of the little form. "A
girl. And she's already wiggling around." Probably cold.

He laid the squirming babe in the blanket he'd
prepared and wrapped both sides around her, then
followed the book's instructions for how to sever the
cord. One thing was certain, he'd never be confused for
a nurse. Hopefully this would be the only time he'd be
called on for this kind of responsibility.

With the babe finally freed, he wrapped the blanket
tighter and lifted her up for Katie to see the little face.

Katie was sitting up, and her own visage glowed
even brighter than the firelight. "She's perfect." Her

tone sounded breathless. And exhausted. "Can I hold her?"

He could only chuckle. "She's yours. And she's remarkable."

He shifted closer to Katie's side, a challenge with such an important bundle in his arms and his leg complaining against the effort. Katie's hands trembled as she reached for her daughter. Was she strong enough to keep from dropping the babe?

She'd been through so much—far more agony than Aaron had ever endured, even when his leg was shattered. And she'd fought with every breath to deliver her daughter.

A warrior, this woman. He could think of no better word.

As he laid the bundle in her arms, he kept his hand just beneath hers until he was certain she had enough strength to hold the babe safely. She stared down at the sweet face, surrounded by blankets. The babe's dark eyes fixed on her mother, and her tiny mouth formed an O.

"Sarah." Katie breathed the name. "You're beautiful."

The little mouth opened wider, as though Sarah was trying to answer.

Katie giggled. "Hello. Will you talk to me?"

Aaron's chest gripped so tight, he could barely breathe. The pair were beautiful. Breathtaking.

But then Katie's body went stiff, curling forward.

"Here. Take her."

She flung Sarah toward him, and he grabbed the bundle just in time.

As he pulled the infant close to his chest, Katie curled around her belly and rolled onto her side away from him. "Oh, why won't it stop?"

This must be that other thing the book spoke of, the passing of the birthing materials. *Lord, why does even this have to bring her pain? Hasn't she endured enough?*

As though little Sarah could feel her mother's discomfort, she began fussing and wiggled her head in the blanket.

He held her in the crook of his arm, tucking her close and bouncing her as he'd seen Doc Micah do with his own child. Aaron had moved out of the clinic a few months after the babe was born, but maybe he'd seen some things that would help Katie and Sarah.

He moved his free hand to Katie's back and rubbed the way she seemed to like.

The moment he touched her, she reached back, her fingers fumbling frantically. Did she want his hand for something? Or did she want him to hand her the stick she'd clutched before?

He moved his hand to where she could reach it if she wanted, and she grasped his fingers, pulling them. He moved forward as she tugged, but then she adjusted her grip on him and simply wrapped her hand around his.

She held tightly, so maybe *he* was taking the place of the stick. But the warmth of her grip, the acceptance in it, warmed all the way up his arm and through his chest. They'd been through one of the hardest ordeals anyone could suffer—at least for her part—and not only had they survived, they had this beautiful babe to show for it.

~

She should be sleeping, but Katie couldn't stop herself from opening her eyes to take in her daughter's face again.

Sarah was precious, from the innocent trust in her eyes when she looked up at Katie to the sweet bow of her lips. Just now, those eyes were closed and her lips moved with each breath that came in and out.

They'd finally figured out nursing after a while of trying. When Sarah's efforts became more frantic, that seemed to be the key that showed them both what was needed. And now that she was content again, this was the chance for both of them to sleep.

Aaron moved over by the wagon, sorting through crates for one that would be the right size for Sarah's bed. He'd been remarkable through it all. Not talking overmuch or asking silly questions that would only frustrate her. He'd simply been there. Rubbing her back, wiping a cold cloth across her brow, everything she needed. And he'd known exactly what to do with

Sarah. He must have studied the book intently while she was caught up in her pains.

In truth, he'd seemed comfortable with her from the first moment he took the babe in his hands. Maybe he had a younger sister who gave him practice.

He turned toward her now, carrying an empty crate. He looked tired—he'd been up all night too.

He bent low beside her, his gaze roaming over Sarah's sleeping form with a softness that made her chest ache. Then his focus lifted to Katie, and that softness remained. "I'll put a blanket in here for a mattress. Do you want her to sleep here now or stay with you?"

She tried for a smile, but her weary muscles didn't manage much. "I don't want to let her go yet."

He nodded. "I wouldn't either." He glanced back toward the fire. "I'll make some warm food you can eat when you're ready. You should sleep if you can though. You need to recover your strength."

She gave a small nod. "I will."

He gave her a look. "Make sure you do. If you want me to hold her so you can rest, just say the word."

Now the smile came of its own accord. "I'll let you know."

And she would. At this point, Aaron Long had more than earned both her trust and the chance to dote over this precious daughter.

For now, though, she snuggled the bundle closer and closed her eyes, letting the exhaustion take over.

*K*atie awoke to something warm beside her, but it wasn't the right warm. Nor in the right place.

She forced her eyelids open through the grogginess and lifted her head. Camp. The fire leapt not far away, but that wasn't the warmth she felt.

The baby.

She came fully awake and reached for the place Sarah had been tucked in the crook of her arm.

Her hand found only an empty blanket.

She twisted to see the source of the warmth pressed against her back. Surely she hadn't moved around so much that she'd pushed her daughter off the blankets onto the cold ground.

Her hand found fur. Not Sarah. The dog.

She nearly slapped him in her urgency, and he yelped and jumped to his feet.

A chuckle drifted from behind her, and she turned to find its source.

Aaron sat propped against a crate, a wad of blanket tucked in the crook of his arm. The pink of Sarah's cheek poked out. The two of them looked so comfortable there, as though this was a familiar position to both of them.

Aaron nodded toward the dog. "I've never seen him get so close to anyone of his own accord. You had the babe snuggled on one side, and he just came over and laid down on the other." He glanced down at the bundle in his arms, his voice a low murmur. "She started to wiggle around, and I didn't want her to wake you, so I thought I'd hold her a while. She must've thought my talk was a bit dull though, because it didn't take her long to go back to sleep."

The burn of tears stung Katie's eyes. He'd taken Sarah just to make her more comfortable. That fact shouldn't make her cry, but layered on top of everything else he'd done... How he'd been there through it all, a silent presence whenever she'd needed him. He'd helped in ways she never expected but appreciated more than she could express.

To cover up her emotion, she turned back to the dog and held out a hand. He stood warily, just out of reach but watching her. "Here, boy. Sorry I disturbed you. You can come back."

She glanced at Aaron. "What's his name?"

His expression turned sheepish. "I call him Barney. Short for Barnacle. He joined up with me not long after I started my last trip. He's never let me touch him, but he stays just out of reach. Never leaves, just like a barnacle on a ship."

She grinned and turned back to the dog. "Barney, huh?" She pulled her hand back to her side. It seemed him eating from her hand the other night might have been a bit more of a wonder than she'd thought. "You can come back and lay down when you're ready."

She snuggled under the blanket again, turning so

she could see Aaron and Sarah. A yawn forced its way out of her mouth, but she did her best to cover it.

Aaron's look was so gentle, it seeped around her with even more warmth than the blankets. "There's ham and corn mush for you. But if you'd rather sleep longer, it will wait."

"You probably need to rest more than I do. Have you lain down at all?" The low gray clouds made it hard to tell what time it was.

"I'll sleep tonight. For now, I'm here to do whatever you need."

She should protest against the words. Insist she care for herself. After all, this was her time to be her own person. To finally make decisions for her and her daughter instead of living under the rule of those placed over her.

But no one had ever treated her with so much care and consideration as Aaron did now. Maybe it would be all right to rest in his help a while longer. Until she gained strength again.

Then she would start her new life. A good life for Sarah.

*❦*

*A*s a gust of wind swept through, Aaron curled the babe closer to himself, tucking the blanket as tight around her face as he dared. Only the little nose and mouth peeked out, her tiny lips parting with each breath.

Such delicate features. Such a fragile life that would extinguish if he did the wrong thing. He'd never had someone so vulnerable depend on him. He'd never had *anyone* depend on him except Nate.

*God, I'm not enough for this. How do I protect her out here with no shelter?*

He eyed the clouds that had been growing thicker and lower all morning. Snow would come soon. He couldn't let Katie and Sarah remain out in the weather. If he used the oilskin covers from the wagon, he could make a tent for them. That would at least keep them dry.

But nothing more than a tent to protect a newborn from a possible blizzard? That wasn't enough.

He looked to Katie, snuggled under her blankets, her face finally relaxed—more so than any other time since he'd first met her.

Would it hurt her to travel in the wagon? He had no notion of whether anything had been damaged inside from the childbirth. But he knew well that a pain as deep as she'd endured could leave lingering effects. A wagon ride would be uncomfortable, he had no doubt. Would it be too much to ask her to endure it?

An abandoned cabin stood a ways down the road. It had likely once been a trapper's winter quarters, since it sat so near a lake. Freighters often stayed overnight there.

The place was about a day and a half's ride away if they took all the usual rest stops and camped overnight. But if they left now and he didn't stop to sleep, he could get them there about this time tomorrow. Cain and Abel'd had a good rest, so they should be able to pull that far without stopping for the night.

He'd have to wake Katie, disturb the peaceful expression in her much-needed sleep. His chest tightened, but he scooted closer to her side, doing his best to keep Sarah from jostling too much.

Katie's face had regained much of the color she'd lost by the end of the delivery, and now her skin looked too perfect, like that of a glass doll. And so beautiful. She was meant for the elegance she must have come from. He'd never been in a ballroom, but he could imagine her dressed up in a sparkling gown, her hair piled in a fancy style and sparkling jewels around her neck. She would be breathtaking.

No more breathtaking than she was now.

He allowed himself a single touch, traced the side of her face with the back of his finger.

Her eyelids lifted, and her gaze met his.

He'd been caught. He could pull his hand away and pretend he never touched her. Ignore the way she made his heart beat faster.

But he didn't. Perhaps it was the intensity in her eyes. No fear there, only...a knowing.

He finished following the line of her face down to the bottom of her jaw, then eased his hand back, wrapping it around Sarah's blankets. "How are you feeling?"

His words seemed to wake her from whatever had connected them for a moment. Her focus dropped to her daughter. "Is she hungry?"

He looked down at the tiny circle of sleeping face. "She's been sleeping a while. I'm trying to keep her warm." He glanced at the sky again. "I think snow will fall in the next day or two. There's a shack down the road a ways that would be better cover than I could make for us here." He studied her face. "Do you think you and Sarah can travel if I make your bed in the back of the wagon again?"

"Of course." She sat upright and started to pull the blankets off her. The blast of cold must have been more than she'd expected, for she tugged them back up to her shoulders.

"If you hold Sarah, I'll get the team ready. You two don't need to get up until I have your bed made in the wagon."

She reached for her daughter, and he eased the bundle into her arms. Their hands brushed in the passing, and it felt far too much like they were truly in this together. Father and mother, working as one to protect and care for this sweet life.

Or maybe that was only in his mind. He'd never wanted a family. But if he'd known it would be like this, that there would be this...this place he could belong...

These people who looked at him like the man they needed...

He eased away and stood before his mind could carry that thought further. He had work to do. If he was ever going to prove himself worthy—even as a simple companion—he had to get them to safety before the weather turned worse.

# CHAPTER 8

*E*ven under cover of the blanket, Katie's breath clouded in front of her face as the wagon bumped and jostled along. She didn't dare lift a corner of the shelter to see if snow still fell outside. It had started hours ago, and with the first flakes, she'd placed one of their blankets like a tent just over her head to keep the wind and wet away from her daughter.

Though Katie hadn't been warm since they started out yesterday, she'd started keeping Sarah tucked under her dress where her body heat should add to the protection of the blankets. It had the extra benefit of making nursing easier, and her daughter shifted between sleeping and eating without having to move far.

Aaron's voice shouted from outside her cover, and the wagon bumped to a stop. Had something happened? Or maybe they'd finally reached the cabin where they would find shelter.

She reached up and moved the side of the blanket so she could see out. White powder sifted in, brushing her face with its icy fingers. The view through the opening only showed falling snow thickening the air. As she widened the opening, she adjusted her position to keep the baby underneath the shelter.

An old cabin stood to the side of the road. It leaned a little, probably thanks to rotting logs. Or maybe the ground beneath it slanted. Either way, would it be safe for them to enter?

"We made it." Aaron's voice sounded rougher than usual as he traipsed along the side of the wagon.

And no wonder, for he'd been awake two days straight, working hard to get them to this place of protection. As soon as they got a fire started and carried in enough blankets and food to last them, she would make sure he slept.

She eased upright, moving carefully so she didn't wake Sarah. She should help Aaron bring things in, but that would require taking her daughter out of the warm cocoon. Either way, she would have to be careful climbing down from the wagon.

As Aaron rounded the back corner of the conveyance, his head disappeared, and he shouted.

Her heart lurched. Had he fallen? She scrambled to the side and peered down.

Aaron lay sprawled in the snow. Groaning as he pushed himself up on one arm.

"Are you hurt?" She had to get down to him. What if he'd broken his leg again?

"I'm all right." But he paused, braced on one elbow. Maybe he couldn't stand.

She rose up and climbed over the rear of the wagon, gripping Sarah with one hand and the wood with the other. The falling snow made the ground slippery, so she moved slowly. She couldn't risk injuring Sarah.

As soon as her feet landed in the thick icy crystals, she spun to Aaron and dropped to her haunches. "Where does it hurt? Your leg?" The dog had approached on the other side, closer than usual, as though ready to help where he could.

"I'm all right." Aaron pushed up to sitting, though the movement clearly pained him.

She placed a hand at his back. Now that he sat upright, he seemed steadier. "Sit for a minute and see if any damage has been done. Is your leg broken?"

He sent her a scowl. "It's not broken. Stop fussing."

She pulled back. Aaron had never spoken to her like that. The tone sounded too much like Neil's. In those early days when she'd tried to get close, he'd rebuffed her with nearly those exact words. *Stop fussing.* So she had.

And now from Aaron. At their core, men really were all the same. Her father. Neil. Even Aaron.

"Katie, I'm sorry. I didn't mean that." Aaron's tone

shifted to apologetic, something Neil's and her father's never had.

She made herself look back at him.

He ran both hands through his hair. "I'm sorry. I just hate that I'm so..." He dropped his hands and found her gaze with his. "I want to be strong. Capable." He nodded to where Sarah squirmed under her gown. "You were so brave during the birth. I wasn't that way with my leg. I let pain in those dark days smother me. I thought I'd put all that behind me. Let God make me new, a better man. But sometimes that darkness closes in again. And I just can't..."

His eyes pleaded with her. For understanding? Maybe for a hand to reach in and pull him out of the shadows.

She could do that. She'd been there herself, and not very long ago.

She reached out and gripped his hand in hers. "I understand the darkness. I've come through it too. In fact, Sarah's birth was the first hard thing I've been able to face without slipping into that despair. I think it's because you were there with me. When things were hardest, you made the pain more bearable."

His eyes softened a little. "I was praying so hard the entire time. God gave you the strength you needed." His gaze dropped again to Sarah's form under her dress. "And a beautiful healthy girl."

His fingers tightened around hers, and his thumb caressed the back of her hand.

The sting of tears rose into her eyes. *Not now.* Why did every nice thing this man did make her want to cry? These were happy tears. Mostly. She just wanted to crawl into his arms and let him hold her.

But that was not a good desire. She needed to be strong.

He must have seen the shift in her expression, for he released her hand. "Let me get up, and I'll make sure the cabin is safe to enter. We need to get you two out of the cold."

As Aaron worked up to standing, she attempted the feat herself. Sarah's wiggling had turned to fussing. She would need to eat again soon, and they had much to do before Katie could focus on her.

No matter how rough this cabin was inside, at least they'd found shelter. A safe place to hide away from the storm.

Maybe Aaron had prayed for this too, and God had listened. She glanced upward at the thick gray sky. *Thank You. If You're up there, thank You for bringing me Aaron.* This man made her feel for the first time in years, like God might actually see her.

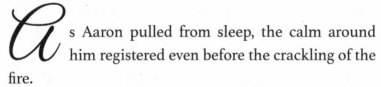

*A*s Aaron pulled from sleep, the calm around him registered even before the crackling of the fire.

No wind.

He forced his mind out of the haze and his eyelids open. Daylight was dimmer than usual. Still early morning?

But a sweep around the room brought everything back. The cabin.

He craned his neck to look for Katie. They'd spread their blankets in front of the little stone hearth at one end of the small building. As soon as he'd made sure Katie, Sarah, and the mules had all they needed— including a blazing fire and plenty of wood to add to it —he'd succumbed to his exhaustion. Only once had he awakened in the night. Katie must have been adding wood all along, for the blaze had been burning bright.

Her blankets lay empty, though mussed.

He sat upright, holding in a groan as his bruises from the fall protested. A movement in the shadows on the other side of the hearth caught his focus. When his eyes finally found her, Katie's sweet smile pulled him fully awake. She sat against the wall, a blanket draped across the front of her. That must mean she was nursing Sarah.

The dog sat on her far side, stretched out against her leg. Ever since Sarah's birth, he often planted himself close, as though the babe's presence soothed him. A feeling Aaron could relate to.

"Did you sleep well?" Katie's voice held such a peaceful cadence, settling through him like a warm drink on a cold day.

"Like a dead man." His voice rumbled with a thick

sleep rasp, so he cleared his throat as he glanced toward the closed door. The place had no windows, but enough of the chinking had fallen from between the logs that daylight peeked through.

He turned back to Katie. "Have you been outside yet?"

She shook her head. "Not since last night. I was asleep until just now when Sarah woke up hungry." She nodded toward the fire. "I made coffee. I wasn't sure if you'd want coffee or tea, but I thought this would help if you're still tired."

He eyed the kettle. "Sounds like just the thing." He stood and used the wall to catch his balance until his weak leg felt secure, then he poured a cup and held it out to Katie.

She shook her head. "Thank you, but not yet. When Sarah's finished, do you think you might"—she rolled her lips between her teeth—"hold her a minute while I go outside."

Heat flushed up his neck, and he pulled the cup back to himself. "Of course. I haven't seen her in nearly a day."

To give Katie some privacy, he ambled toward the door and peeked outside. He needed to check on Cain and Abel, but that could wait until she'd finished with her personal affairs. He'd left the mules under a thick stand of trees where they would be mostly sheltered from the snow, but now he should move them to water. They might not be able to find grazing with the ground covered so thickly, but maybe there would be a place shallow enough they could dig down to grass.

The door stuck when he first tried to push, but more pressure helped it break loose, and he forced the wood open the rest of the way. The snow came up at least mid-thigh—just about to the spot where a metal plate held his leg bone together.

He swallowed down a knot of worry. How would he ever get the wagon through this mess? Being the first snow of the year, it was light and fluffy, hard for the mules to plow through and not easy for the wagon to maneuver the slopes with chains on the wheels.

A glance upward showed a gray sky. Not the low thick clouds that portended more snow—*thank you, Lord, for that*—but no sunshine and warm temperatures to melt this sea of white either.

*This would be a great time for a warm Chinook wind, Father.*

They would need to stay in this cabin today at least. After he settled the mules, he could walk to the next slope and see how the road looked. Maybe tomorrow after the snow melted a little and re-froze, the road would be fit for travel. He couldn't risk Katie and Sarah's safety.

Yet he also had to get this load to Settler's Fort. For that matter, he had to get Katie and Sarah to Settler's Fort. They needed a warm house and Doc Micah's attention. And now that the first snow had fallen, who knew when the next would come and how deep it would pile. He had to get them to better shelter before they risked being snowed in here all winter.

Rustling sounded from behind him, and he glanced back as Katie stood and pulled the blanket off her shoulder. He closed the door, scraping it across the snow again, then turned and moved back to the fire.

Katie snugged the babe's blanket tighter, and Aaron moved in beside her.

Sarah's wide dark eyes stared up at them both. She closed her pale lids and opened her mouth in a wide yawn.

"Look at how precious." Katie's voice held so much love, his chest tightened.

"She is that." He'd never imagined he'd fall so quickly for a tiny baby, yet this one's innocence and sweet personality were impossible not to adore.

Katie held out the bundle and he tucked Sarah in the curve of his arm, a little upright so she could see the world around her.

"I'll just be a minute." Katie reached for her coat.

"No need to rush. It's cold out there though. Better bundle up."

When Katie left the cabin, Barney stayed inside, padding at Aaron's heels as he sauntered around the room, letting the wide-eyed babe see anything she might be interested in. "There's our stack of firewood. I'll bring in more after I see to the mules. And here's our food pack. I should get some water heating for corn mush. Maybe later today we can have meat stew. I'll bet your mama would like that." Katie needed meals with substance to regain her strength.

He'd just managed to fill the pot with snow from outside the door and carry it back to heat beside the fire when Katie returned.

"I can take her now." She looked fresher than when she'd left, her nose and cheeks red from the cold.

He wouldn't have minded keeping the babe, but the mules needed him more just now. When he handed Sarah back to her mother, their hands brushed again, as they had so many times now. Her touch no longer made him nervous. Now it steadied him, made him want to lean in to keep the connection.

But he had to pull back once Katie had a firm hold. "I was just about to put corn mush on to heat, but I need to move the mules to water and grazing. If I start food cooking, will you watch over it?"

As he spoke the words, he wanted to pull them back. He shouldn't assume she knew how to prepare such a plain dish over a hearth fire. She'd likely had a chef who fixed fancy meals. But she'd shown a fair hand at cooking so far, and mush took little talent.

She nodded and offered a smile that showed no trepidation. "Of course."

He reached for the corn meal and stirred the right amount into the melting snow, then positioned it near the fire. "Meat stew might be nice for later in the day. I'll bring in the rest of the cooking supplies when I'm done with the mules." He took up his gloves and coat, then pushed up to his feet.

"We'll be here." The gentle tone of her voice brought his gaze back to her.

The way she stood there, little Sarah in her arms, the two of them smiling at him as though whether he returned or not mattered to them... What would it be like to have a family like this to come back to every time?

With effort, he turned toward the door. It opened easier this time, and he stepped out into an icy breeze. The ache in his thigh turned to sharper pain as he lifted his knees high through the snow.

The wagon stood like a whitecapped abandoned rig in the place he'd pulled off the road. He trudged around the cabin to the trees where the land sloped down to the lake.

Cain brayed in greeting as Aaron approached them, then Abel joined him.

"You hungry, boys?" The mules had stayed in the rope fence he'd strung when they arrived. They were both likely so tired from pulling for nearly twenty-four hours, they didn't have the desire to push out.

He attached a rope to Abel's halter, then untied the fence to let both animals through. Cain wouldn't wander far from his brother, unlike his namesake from the book of Genesis.

He led Abel out, then Cain charged ahead, trotting out through the snow with a high step. Beside him, even

Abel took a few sideways steps as he tried to follow. The elder mule settled in once they reached the thicker snow, and together they trudged toward the lake.

A thin layer of ice coated the water, but Cain had already pawed a hole through the frozen mass and was drinking deeply by the time Aaron got there. As Abel joined him, Aaron dropped the rope to let them gulp all they wanted while he tested the ground beneath the snow for grass.

The white powder was too thick for him to dig through with his feet, so he hiked back to the trees and grabbed a branch sturdy enough for the job.

His arms were stronger than his legs, so he dug down quickly. There was grass beneath the snow, but the effort to find it would be so hard, the mules wouldn't get enough to fill their bellies. He'd have to add to the corn he gave them each day. He'd planned to ration it so there would be enough for a delay here and the rest of the trip to Settler's Fort.

One more reason to get back on the road as soon as they could.

He hobbled through his tracks back to the mules and came alongside Abel. The animals had stopped drinking, and Abel swung his head around to greet Aaron. He patted the mule's shoulder with one hand and held out the other for him to nuzzle.

Just as Abel placed his nose in Aaron's glove, the mule stumbled. On the other side, Cain pushed against him as he spun away from the water.

Abel knocked into Aaron's weak leg, pushing him sideways. He couldn't catch his balance quickly enough, and he tumbled to the ground on his backside.

One of the mules squealed, and Abel's body plunged toward him. Something hard struck the side of Aaron's head.

The pain registered first. Then the blackness.

And nothing else.

# CHAPTER 9

"Settle down, Sarah. Everything is all right." Katie adjusted her daughter so she would finally stop fussing and nurse.

Everything *was* all right. Surely.

But why hadn't Aaron returned yet? She'd dozed after Sarah went to sleep, though she hadn't meant to. She'd only awakened because her daughter fussed.

The mush he'd left heating by the fire had scorched, its aroma tainting the smell of wood smoke to something sour.

If Aaron had returned while she slept, he would have pulled the food away from the fire. She had no doubt about that.

She must have been asleep an hour at least, maybe longer. Did he need help out there? He'd said he would try to find grazing too, so perhaps he'd had to take the mules a long way. Or perchance he was disassembling the contents of the wagon to find items to make this cabin more livable.

Or maybe something awful had happened. Possibly he'd slipped in the ice again and really had broken his leg this time.

She had to go out and find him. But Sarah also needed to eat, and she wouldn't be stalled much longer. Maybe half the length of a normal feeding would suffice until they found Aaron.

Every minute Sarah nursed made Katie's body coil tighter. Even the little one squirmed, though she ate with hungry determination. This babe had connected so easily with Aaron, perhaps she sensed something was wrong with him.

That was a silly thought, of course, but they had to go find him. Maybe she could wrap blankets around the two of them and let Sarah continue nursing while she walked.

Once she'd done that and had the two of them as warm as she could manage, she pushed open the door and stepped out into the whipping wind. Barney followed her, staying behind in her tracks.

The wagon stood where they'd left it, the thick layer of snow that covered it undisturbed. The wind had blown snow into Aaron's tracks, but she could still make out each dip where he'd broken through the high powder.

As soon as she rounded the rear of the cabin, the two mules came into view. The pair stood near each other, heads down in the snow. One of them pawed the ground. Maybe they'd found grazing.

As she started toward them, she raised her voice to call out. "Aaron?"

The sound echoed over the open space, and the mules lifted their heads. One of them brayed—Abel, maybe? He wasn't quite as stout as the more energetic brother. His call pierced the air, resounding as her voice had.

In its wake, an eerie silence settled. Even the wind had ceased.

Her feet crunched in the snow, and her dress plowed through the white as she lifted each leg high and kicked the fabric forward. Her stockings were already wet, and the cold was seeping down into her boots.

Aaron might have frostbite, as long as he'd been out here.

He hadn't answered her call, and she glanced around in every direction as she walked. "Aaron? Where are you?"

The wind picked up again, whistling in her ears. Sarah stirred at her chest, and she adjusted the babe as she kept her forward march.

All she could think to do was follow Aaron's tracks, though out here, the wind had filled them even more than by the cabin.

As she neared the mules, a dark spot to the side snagged her attention.

*No!*

She raised her knees higher to run toward the form, even as a cry welled in her throat. *No!*

Aaron lay in the snow, his body motionless. Was that...? Crimson smeared the white near his head.

When she reached him, his eyes were open but his body motionless. Emotion clogged her chest so much she couldn't breathe. Was he dead? Flashes came of Neil's blank expression as he lay in a pool of blood, his eyes open and lifeless.

*No! God, he can't... You can't...*

But then his eyes turned toward her, his head shifting a little.

Relief swept through her, and she sucked a breath as she dropped to her knees by his side.

His gaze followed her, but his eyes didn't seem focused. Was that from pain? Or damage to his mind? Or simply the numbing cold?

She laid a hand on his shoulder. "What happened? Where are you hurt?"

His eyes narrowed. "Abel. Knocked me." He lifted his hand slowly to his head. But even before he touched the bloodied hair, his face twisted in a sharp wince.

She leaned over him to see the far side of his head, touching his temple and turning him a little for a better view. The blood matted his hair so thickly that she couldn't see the wound. She needed to get him out of the cold before she cleaned it.

Pulling back, she studied the length of him. "Can you sit up?"

He didn't speak, just started to turn on his side so he could push upright. A groan rumbled out, and he flopped back to the snow. "My leg."

She honed her gaze on the left leg he limped on. But it was the right limb his hands moved to, clutching the upper part.

"What happened? What's wrong with it?" Where he touched showed no sign of injury, though farther down his trousers were torn—and wet from the snow.

He struggled to get his hands beneath him so he could sit up, this time not trying to roll onto his side. With her free hand, she pushed his back until he sat up with his legs straight before him.

He touched his right calf with both hands, and his breath clouded the air around him. "God, no. Not again." The words groaned out, ending in a cough, a deep rattling sound that rose up from his chest.

"We need to get you to the cabin. Is there a chance you can walk?" Or was the leg broken?

His mouth turned grim. "I'll crawl back if I have to."

She couldn't let him do that. Scanning the area, she caught sight of the mules. "Could you ride one of them to the cabin? Or maybe I could hook them to the wagon."

He shook his head. "The wagon wouldn't make it through this loose snow." He looked to the trees. "See if you can find two sturdy sticks, a little shorter than I am."

She rose and pointed for Barney to stay. "Take care of him, boy." The dog dipped his head as though accepting the charge, then dropped to his haunches at Aaron's side. She turned and started toward the pines. Aaron likely had experience with walking sticks. This would be the best way.

By the time she found two branches that might work, Sarah had finished nursing and Katie moved her up to her shoulder to burp. But keeping the babe covered from the cold while carrying both sticks proved more than she could manage.

Should she take Sarah back into the cabin and lay her in her crate bed? Sarah would be out of the wind and Katie would have both hands free to help Aaron. She had a feeling she would need that.

Leaving the walking sticks, she hurried through the snow to the cabin. She had to get Aaron inside. Already, his exposure to the cold and wet might be enough to threaten his life.

Sarah stared up at her with wide eyes as she laid her in the crate. Those eyes were so beautiful. Alert.

"Stay here where you'll be safe, my sweet. I'll be back soon with Aaron." As she tucked the blanket over her daughter's body, one more thought slipped out. "Pray for him. He might need a miracle."

Of course, the babe couldn't pray for Aaron, but he needed someone to. Katie turned and headed out the door again. Could she be the one? She and God hadn't spoken in so very long. Not since the trip west.

*God, I'm not asking for me but for Aaron. Protect him. Don't let anything bad be wrong with him. Please, don't let me lose him.*

With that last thought, a surge of panic forced its way up her throat, closing off her ability to breathe or even swallow. She couldn't lose another man she was depending on. Not again. This was why she wanted to take control of her life. Not to rely on others who determined her fate.

But it was more than that. The thought of losing Aaron... He'd come to mean far too much to her in such a short time. His kindness. His steadiness. The way he looked at her like he really saw her. Like what he found inside didn't repulse him.

She couldn't lose Aaron.

With that thought flowing strength through her limbs, she ran through her earlier tracks to the trees, lifting her skirts so she could raise her knees high.

In the woods, she grabbed up the walking sticks and started toward Aaron. He still sat up where she'd left him, but his shoulders had collapsed and his head hung in his hands as though he didn't have the strength in his neck to keep it upright. A knock hard enough to bring all that blood had likely left a significant headache.

She dropped to her knees by his side, but he didn't

lift his head to acknowledge her. "Do you think you can stand?"

"I might need help." His voice sounded dull, and speaking brought another round of coughs. He turned away from her as he kept one hand gripping his head while the other wrapped around his middle.

Her own insides ached with his pain. She pressed a hand to his back, and as soon as he finished coughing, she said, "Let's get you up."

He reached out. "Hand me the sticks. As I pull up, you might need to lift me from behind. My left leg isn't as strong as it once was, and I don't think I can use the right one at all."

After helping him place the poles, she moved around to his back. He lifted himself by his arms, struggling to get even halfway up. She placed her hands on each of his sides to help him, and a grunting wheeze slipped from him. The tendons of his neck stood out as he strained, but finally he pulled all the way up to standing.

She moved to his side, but with the walking sticks in the way, she couldn't do much to support him. He stood on his left foot, his right one resting out in front a little. He seemed to bear most of his weight on the walking sticks.

He moved forward with both poles, then swung his body through the snow. His legs plowed furrows through the white, and Aaron let out a strangled sound. His leg must truly be broken to hurt like that.

She moved around in front of him. "Let me move the snow out of your way before you come through." He was already taking the trail she'd walked through, but she used her boots to clear away more crystals from the path, making the trench deeper so his injured leg didn't drag as much.

He followed behind her, and every time she looked back, his face was a little paler, his jaw locked tighter. He might lose consciousness from the pain before they reached the cabin.

She focused on clearing the walkway, but Aaron slowed as they progressed. When she reached the cabin door, he still hadn't rounded the rear corner.

She strode back to find him. If only she could help more.

There he was, and from the way his face twisted in pain, each step took all he had left. She couldn't even wrap an arm around his waist, for that would get in the way of his walking sticks. She placed a light hand on his back and followed just behind. "You can do it. We're almost there." *God, now would be a good time to help him.*

# CHAPTER 10

Once Katie helped Aaron hobble inside the cabin, she scurried ahead to prepare his blankets. He didn't lower himself onto them, though, but landed beside them on the hard dirt floor, his sticks falling away with a clatter.

He groaned as he laid back on the ground.

She dropped to his side. "Do you want to move on to the blankets? They'll be warmer."

He took in ragged breaths as he lay with his eyes closed. "Wet."

She scanned the length of him. His clothing was soaked, and his body had begun to tremble. She needed to build up the fire more, then get him wrapped in blankets. He had to get out of those wet clothes, but she couldn't help him with that, and if his leg was broken, he likely couldn't manage the bottom half by himself.

But perhaps they could change his shirt. That would help some.

She turned to look for the pack where he kept his personal items. There, by the food. "We need to put you in a dry shirt. Do you want to find one or should I?"

"You." His eyes were still closed, and pain lines creased around them. Even his voice shook with his shivers.

She untied the pack and flipped the cover open. The navy wool shirt he often wore lay near the top. She grabbed it out, then prepared it to slip over his head.

But first she had to get Aaron out of his wet garment.

She reached for the buttons near his neck. She only had to imagine herself a nurse, helping an urgently ill patient. That *was* the case, after all.

Yet as her fingers brushed his chest, she couldn't push away the attraction that made her own hands tremble. She could so easily flatten her palms to his shirt and feel the thick muscle beneath.

She couldn't let her mind linger on that thought. Aaron needed to get warm.

With the four buttons at his neck unfastened, she pulled back and eyed him. "Can you sit up to take off the shirt?"

His breathing stilled, and he lifted his head, then braced his elbows on the ground and worked his way up to sitting. Every shift took an incredible amount of strength. When he finally sat upright, his breathing started again. This time light and raspy. "Take off."

Moving to his back, she gripped the bottom hem of his shirt and pulled upward. An undershirt tried to come too, but she tugged it back down.

As she worked the outer garment up and over his head, he let out a strangled moan. The collar must have scraped his wound.

"I'm so sorry." She mumbled the words through the knot in her throat. The last thing she wanted was to hurt him worse.

She took more care removing the undershirt, its fabric just as soaked through as the outer garment. Once she pulled it off, she tried not to look at his skin as she reached for the dry shirt.

But with her senses so alive, she couldn't stop herself. Even from the back, his muscles flexed with every shift of his movement. His torso tapered to a lean waist. This man was in the peak of condition. In his prime, despite the limp that he didn't let hold him back.

She forced herself to focus on not scraping the side of his head as she pulled this new shirt in place. At last, she had him ready to lie down again. "Before you rest, let me move your bed underneath you."

"Trousers wet." He sat with his head lolling forward and his shoulders slumped.

She pulled one end of his bed pallet to where he could lay back on it. "They'll have to stay wet. But we need to get you warm and wrapped up. Can you scoot over onto this?"

As he lifted himself over, she helped shift his injured right leg. He sucked in a sharp breath but didn't cry out this time.

Still, when he slumped back to lie on the blanket, what color had returned to his face before now leached out.

He met her gaze. "You're going to need to cut through both layers of pants, all the way up to the knee. See how the swelling is. See if the bone broke through. It needs to be splinted, but we might have to set it first."

The color of her own face must match his. Set his broken leg? Her heart pounded, and her breaths came in tiny shards.

"Please, Katie." His gaze turned earnest, but then another coughing fit broke through his focus, and he turned aside as his shoulders shook.

With her own chest aching, she moved to her carpet bag and pulled out Neil's hunting knife. The blade should be sharp enough to slice the fabric easily. But first, she should pile blankets on Aaron's upper half so he could start to get warm.

She gathered the extra covers, then all of her own quilts. As she passed by Sarah's crate, her daughter stared up at her, as though questioning what was happening. "We have to get Aaron warm." She kept her voice low. "Keep praying for him." A reminder to herself, of course.

*God, help Aaron. Take away his pain. Show me what to do for him.*

As she spread the blankets over Aaron, he grabbed them and pulled them close to his shivering body. "Th-thank you."

She moved to his leg and knelt, taking up the knife again. "I'm going to cut your trouser leg now. I'll be careful."

He didn't answer, so she grasped the hem and adjusted her hold on the knife. The blade was long and thick, which made the work awkward. But once she'd pierced the fabric the first time, she used a sawing motion to work her way up the leg. As he'd said, a pair of woolen underpants lay beneath, just as wet as all the other garments had been.

Once she'd cut the outer layer to his knee, she started on the next. These fit his leg much closer, but she pulled them out as much as she could to keep from slicing his skin.

As she cut, she tried to make out anything unusual on his leg beneath. The limb was far more substantial than she'd expected. No puny leg this. Yet was that all muscle, or swelling from his injury too?

Once she finished slicing the fabric to the same place as the other, she laid down the knife and tugged both sides apart. Her chest tightened.

She could more clearly see the definition of his calf, but near the base of the thicker muscle, another puffiness rose higher than the rest.

"Do you see the bone?" Aaron's voice rasped, but at least it didn't tremble any longer, though his body still shook.

"There's no bone protruding. There's some swelling though. Right here." She touched a light finger to the place.

His leg jerked. "That's the spot. There's no break in the skin?"

She moved her head to see underneath. "No." That was good, right?

"Is there a bend or a twist in the leg? Does it look crooked?"

She rose up on her knees so she could see from the top down. "I don't...think so. It's hard to know for sure with the swelling, but the other side looks straight."

He released a long breath. "Maybe it doesn't need setting then. Might be just a crack. But we need to splint and wrap it to keep the crack from spreading."

She blew out her own spent air, forcing out her tension with it. "All right."

Surely she could do that. For Aaron, she would do anything.

As she shifted so she could see his face nearly buried with the blankets, the ache in her chest tightened. She had to get him more comfortable. If she could take this pain on herself, she would.

But she couldn't. It was her job to act. To call on everything she'd ever learned to help this man who'd become far more important to her than she'd ever meant to allow.

~

*a*aron's head pounded, but he couldn't tell if it was from the gash behind his ear or the urgency that pressed through him. The darkness he was doing his best to ward off didn't help matters.

Lying here in the dim cabin, the pain in his leg radiating through the entire limb and his head aching, felt too much like those dark days when he was recovering from the gunshot wound. At least they had no laudanum here. He could still taste its sweetness, that desperation for more, to fall under its spell. To find the hint of relief it brought. His addiction had nearly ruined not only his own life, but Nate's and Laura's too.

The scrape of the wood door sounded behind him, and he turned toward the light. The dog padded in first, then Katie stepped in with Sarah in a sling across her front. The two of them brought in even more sunshine than what shone through the open doorway.

They'd become the brightness in his days, both of them. The only rays of light in the darkness since the accident. How many days had it been? Two, maybe three. Maybe thirty.

Too long. He had to get Katie and Sarah to Settler's Fort. And the supplies in the wagon.

He felt so helpless, lying here with the pain wrapping around him. But he had to be strong. For them. *God, help me.*

"Brr." Katie unfastened the buttons of his coat, which she was wearing. She'd taken to donning it since the bigger size wrapped all the way around her and the baby. And he didn't need it, lying beside the fire. "The sun is warm, but that wind still makes it so cold."

As he worked his elbows underneath himself to sit up, the pounding in his head felt like an ax splitting wood. Blow after blow.

"Let me help you." Katie scrambled to his side, reaching with her free hand to push him up.

He gritted his teeth, partly against the pain and partly to keep from snapping at her. He hated being helpless. Hated needing her to sweep in and rescue him. And even more, hated feeling resentful.

*God, You have to help me.* The Lord had pulled him from this mire once, but it had been a hard battle. He couldn't let himself get so deeply entrenched again.

Once he sat upright, he turned sideways on the blanket so he could lean against the wall. His chest heaved as he worked to catch his breath from the effort, but he tried not to let it show.

Katie turned to put more logs on the fire. Now was the time to talk to her about moving on. "Katie."

She tossed the log into the fire, raising a cloud of sparks, before she straightened and turned to him. "Yes?"

He couldn't meet the directness of her gaze, so he

shot a look toward the closed cabin door. "You said the sun's bright today?"

"Finally. It's still cold with the wind though. Do you want to try to go outside?" She started to pull his coat off.

He raised a hand to stop her. Shaking his head only worsened the pounding. "We need to get moving. If the sun's out, maybe it's melting the snow on the road enough that we could get through."

Her brow lined, and her hands moved to cradle Sarah's sling. "You're not well enough to travel. Even if I do the hard parts, bouncing in the wagon all day will be too painful for you. It might damage your leg more too."

It would hurt, he had no doubt about that. But he couldn't hold Katie and Sarah back. "We have to get to Settler's Fort before more snow comes. With another storm, the road might be impassable until spring." He finally met her gaze. "You and Sarah need the doctor. You need to be in a house where the wind won't blow through the cracks, where you'll be warm and dry with people around to help you. And Settler's Fort needs what's in the wagon."

He let out a long breath. "I can't do it without your help though." Those words scraped like a knife as he spoke them. "I can drive, but I don't know that I can hitch the team."

Her lower lip slipped between her teeth as she hesitated. "Of course I'll help, but let's wait a few more days. I'll look for a willow tree by the river so the bark can get rid of your headaches." She'd used the last of her supply to make tea for him, and she'd already gone out to look once before.

"I don't want you out in the cold for me. Not for something that's not absolutely necessary. Besides, we can't wait. The minute the roads are passable, we need to start out. Another snow could come anytime."

In her sling, Sarah waved her arms, pressing against the confines of the cloth. Katie swayed, bouncing a little to calm the babe, though Katie's face looked anything but peaceful as she mulled over his words.

The urge to hold that tiny bundle tightened around him. Sarah soothed his nerves when they turned most raw, and maybe freeing Katie's hands would help her in at least a small way. He reached out, and Katie extracted Sarah's wiggling form from the sling, then handed her over.

As he took the babe, cradling her close, meeting her wide eyes, the warmth that settled through him pushed away some of the darkness. *Thank You for bringing these two to me.*

"How do we know when the road's ready?" Katie's voice pulled him back to the struggle of reality.

He glanced toward the door again. "It'd be best if at least a foot of it has melted. I'm hoping it's packed down a bit more too. I'll go out and check soon." He just needed another minute with this sweet babe to bolster his energy.

# CHAPTER 11

*K*atie reminded herself to breathe as she approached Abel with the rope. She'd managed to move the mules to new grazing each day after his injury, but harnessing them to the wagon would be an entirely different matter.

"Here, boy." She worked to keep her voice from trembling when she grasped his rope halter. Her cold hands fumbled as she knotted the lead rope. Thankfully, the mule stood quietly while she worked. Aaron had said Cain might not be as easy.

*One at a time. Don't borrow trouble.*

Did the animals sense her nervousness? These two didn't seem as rambunctious as Neil's horse had been, but that wiry animal had pushed her around every time she'd had to manage him. She'd actually been thankful when he escaped the fence in the night after Neil's death.

And these two were so much larger. They'd done a great deal of damage to Aaron without even trying. She couldn't let herself get hurt too, not when Sarah and Aaron depended on her.

Squaring her shoulders, she tugged Abel's rope. "Come."

He obliged, walking beside her as she trudged through the icy snow toward the wagon. She'd already laid out the harness, and Aaron waited there to instruct her on how to fasten the team. He'd said once Abel was in place, Cain would be easier to manage.

As they rounded the corner of the cabin and came into view of the wagon, Abel shook his head and snorted. She startled before she could stop herself.

The mule wasn't acting out, just blowing out a breath. She released her own pent-up air, trying to force some of the tension from her chest at the same time. Aaron was watching her. The last thing she wanted was for him to see this weakness.

She didn't meet his gaze as she led Abel past him, just kept her shoulders squared and her stride steady. In truth, she had to keep moving to stay up with the mule's lanky legs. Aaron could have never managed this with his walking sticks.

Once she halted Abel in front of the wagon, Aaron called to her. "That's it. Now place a hand on his chest and back him a step so the harness will reach."

When she touched the mule's chest, he moved backward immediately. "Good boy."

One step at a time, Aaron talked her through how to position the leathers and fasten each buckle. When he hobbled forward and started to help, she pointed a finger at him. "Get away from that, Aaron Long. This is my job."

His mouth pinched, and he turned and limped back to where he'd stood before. She'd meant it as a light-hearted jest, the way she and Aaron had come to banter these last few days. But he'd clearly not taken it that way.

Of course he wouldn't. No man would accept such blatant disrespect. Neil might've slapped her for speaking to him so. In truth, she never would've attempted to banter with Neil.

Once she'd secured Abel, she turned to Cain. He'd followed them up and was pawing through the snow near the cabin. He allowed her to fasten the rope to his halter, but when she tugged for him to follow, he shook his head and snorted.

"You have to take a firmer hand with him. He needs to feel for certain you mean what you're asking of him."

She tightened her grip on the rope and pulled harder. "I mean what I'm asking." She growled just loud enough for the mule to hear, and he seemed to under-stand her, for he turned and started the direction she pulled him.

Getting him in position beside Abel proved a little harder, but with Aaron's instructions, she managed to accomplish it. When she began fastening buckles, Cain blew out a long breath and dropped his head, as though resigning himself to his fate. She didn't relax, though, until she'd finished the final strap.

She glanced over the team's backs at Aaron. "Is that it?"

He nodded. "Let's get Sarah, and we'll head out."

A thrill surged through her as she strode back around the animals and toward Aaron. She'd done it. She'd harnessed both mules, all by herself. With Aaron talking her through each step, of course. So really, they'd done it together.

She clapped her hands as she approached him, and she couldn't help a grin. "We did it." Barney gave a joyful yip from where he sat at Aaron's side.

Aaron's own mouth finally formed a smile, and the sadness that had taken over his eyes these past days eased. "So we did."

When he opened one arm, she stepped into it, tucking herself against his side in a way that felt so natural. He wrapped both arms around her, pulling her closer. She slipped her hands around his waist, careful not to dislodge the walking sticks propped under his arms. The warmth, the security in his hold... She'd never felt so protected. So appreciated.

Her head fit perfectly against his shoulder, and she rested there. Did he feel the thunder of her pulse, being so near him?

A new kind of tension filled the air, slipping through her body. Did he mean anything more by this hug than a quick congratulations? They'd become friends—good friends—through all they'd endured in the short time they'd known each other. But could he possibly feel even a part of the attraction that coursed through her veins every time she was around him?

His hold loosened, his hands moving to her sides as he pulled her back enough that she could look in his face. His eyes had darkened so much she couldn't look away from them. The admiration there...could it be real?

And when his gaze dropped to her lips, a thrill slipped through her body. Everything in her wanted him to kiss her. This man who'd rescued her from the side of the road in a deserted wilderness, who'd helped bring her daughter to life and took joy in simply holding and talking to the babe. He'd proven the kind of man he was in so many ways, and she'd admired him from afar.

But now... When he lowered his mouth to hers, she returned his kiss with fervor. Melding her lips to his, slipping her hands up to his neck, through his hair.

At first, his kiss seemed tentative. Waiting for her response. Even when she gave herself into the act, he held back.

Then something broke loose inside him and he took her mouth with a hunger she'd never felt from a man. Not even when Neil grew forceful.

Yet even in his intensity, Aaron didn't push. He gave. He put his full self into the kiss, giving and giving as though he would never have the chance again.

A cry finally broke through her awareness. The tiny wail of a newborn.

She pulled back, struggling for breath. She had to get to Sarah. They'd left her asleep in her crate, but she must have awakened hungry.

Before she pulled out of Aaron's arms though, she met his gaze once more. His eyes had darkened to that midnight blue that usually concealed their depths, except this time they hid nothing from her. Not the intensity of what he felt for her.

He leaned in and brushed a final kiss across her lips, then pulled back enough for his breath to caress her. "Go get that sweet baby." The huskiness in his voice sent a shiver all the way through her.

She reached up for her own final kiss, then forced herself to pull away. It took all her willpower to leave his arms and hurry into the cabin.

$\sim$

Katie eyed Aaron as the team maneuvered the downward slope. He sat slumped on the bench, his arms wrapped around himself and his head lolling a little to the side. He couldn't be asleep, for when she ducked her head to peer into his face, his eyes were open. Glassy, but open.

They'd been on the road nearly two full days now,

and Aaron seemed to grow worse with every hour. She'd stopped talking to him, for every time he tried to speak, the words dissolved into a coughing fit. Sometimes, the rasp of his breathing rose even over the jingle of harness and swish of the wagon wheels in the snow.

He needed to be tucked in a warm bed with a cozy fire burning nearby and a cup of echinacea tea with honey. Should she stop early for the night to get him out of this wind?

There would be no more cabin along the way to take cover in, but last night she'd cleared snow from a patch of ground beside the wagon, which protected them from the worst of the wind. She'd even managed to start a campfire using his tinderbox to light the spark, thanks to his encouraging direction each step of the way.

In another couple hours, it'd be time to stop for their second night on the trail. She'd thought managing the team and steering the wagon up and down slopes and around tight mountainside corners would be the hardest part of this journey. Or maybe keeping Sarah warm and protected from the elements. But they'd used sticks to form a curved frame over Sarah's crate, then draped blankets to protect her from the wind. She slept peacefully in the little shelter they'd created.

When Katie needed to nurse her, Aaron took over the reins, but the last two times, he'd seemed to barely have the strength to guide the team. She wasn't sure she dared let him attempt it again.

He should lie down in the back of the wagon. She'd tried to send him there several times today, but he'd refused. She should make him go now.

But what if she needed an extra set of hands to care for Sarah? And though she'd learned a great deal about how to maneuver the rig in these snow-covered mountains, sometimes Aaron offered advice on a situation she never would've known she needed.

He didn't look like he even saw the trail ahead though.

As soon as they reached a spot level enough to halt the team, she pulled hard on the reins. "Ho, Abel. Ho, Cain." It took much of her weight to slow the mules as they used their bodies to stop the wagon.

Once they halted, she set the brake and turned to Aaron. He hadn't moved, and his bleary gaze still stared forward. The rasp of his breathing sounded louder now, but its steadiness eased the fear building in her chest. At least he was alive, though his eyes looked nearly lifeless.

She reached over Sarah's crate and placed a hand on his shoulder. "Aaron. Let's move you to the back where you can lie down."

He turned his head with a movement achingly slow. "All right."

He didn't get down, though, so she dismounted on her side, gripping tight to the wagon so she wouldn't slip on the icy wood. The mules stood with their heads down as she walked by them, and she rubbed each of their muzzles when she passed. "Rest a minute, fellas. I need to help Aaron. Pray for him." Why did she keep asking incapable creatures to pray?

When she'd begged the Almighty to keep Aaron alive and help her find him that day, both of those requests had been granted. Maybe God would hear this petition too. For Aaron. Surely He loved Aaron.

*God, heal him. Let me get him to this Settler's Fort town in time. Don't let him die here on the trail.* Giving voice to that thought, even in her mind, raised a surge of panic within her.

She couldn't lose Aaron. He wasn't just another man she depended on. Slowly but surely, he'd won her heart. The heart she'd never intended to give a man. But he'd proven himself worthy of her love.

She couldn't lose him.

When she reached Aaron's side, she pulled his walking sticks from where he'd tucked them under the bench, then gripped his arm. "Come down and I'll help you back to the bed."

Like a wooden doll, he turned his upper body toward her. Even that action brought on a series of coughs that doubled him over, his arms around his middle.

*Help him, God.* Her entire body ached to see Aaron like this.

When he stopped coughing, she climbed onto the wagon step and lifted Aaron's splinted leg, turning the lower half of his body. If only he were a child, she could carry him back to the rear of the wagon, then tuck him in where he could be warm.

But though he was a grown man, he still needed her help.

At last, he gathered enough strength and awareness to climb down, and she guided him, helping him find balance with the walking sticks once he reached the ground. With those poles, she couldn't tuck herself under his arm, but she kept up a steady string of encouragement as she walked beside him. "You're going to feel better soon. Once you rest and get warm, you'll gain strength back. Then we'll be at Settler's Fort, and the doctor can help make you all better."

Something twinged in her spirit. Couldn't God make him better without the doctor's care? She should tell Aaron she'd been praying. Give him hope.

Once she'd helped him climb up the back of the wagon and collapse onto the blanket there, she covered him with all the remaining quilts they had. Only his eyes peered out, and as he stared at her, they didn't appear as glassy as before. More exhausted perhaps, but aware.

She stroked a tuft of hair away from his eyes. "You're going to get better, Aaron Long. I've been praying, and you're going to get better."

Something in his expression changed, brightening his eyes a little. The blanket shifted, and his hand slipped out, reaching for hers. She gripped his gloved fingers with her own.

He squeezed tighter than she'd have thought he had the strength for. Then his voice came through the blankets, muffled but definitely clear enough to understand. "I love you, Katie Barlow. You're the light God sent to keep my darkness away."

The sharp burn of tears sprang to her eyes, and she brought her other hand so she could cling to Aaron with both—with all she had. "I feel the same way. You make me hope for things I never thought possible."

Another cough overtook him—it was a wonder he'd been able to say so much already without coughing.

When the heaves subsided, she lifted his hand to her mouth and pressed a kiss there, then tucked it back under the blankets. "Sleep and get better. I'll get us to Settler's Fort as soon as I can."

# CHAPTER 12

*H*ad Aaron given her the wrong directions?
Katie leaned forward to peer through
the falling snow at the path in front of the mules. This
didn't even seem to be a road. She was simply guiding
the team around the trees in this scattered wood. With
snow covering the ground, she had no idea what lay
beneath.

Before they'd left camp that morning, Aaron had
whispered their route in a hoarse tone in between
coughs. His brother's cabin lay off the main road
through a sparse wood. She'd found the marker to
know when to leave the road, but were they still going
the right direction? She'd been navigating these trees
for more than a quarter hour now. Maybe she'd missed
the cabin.

She glanced back at Aaron but only caught a
glimpse of the blanket that cocooned him before she

had to look back at the land ahead to guide the team around a cluster of trees.

Should she stop and ask him if he recognized anything around them? He'd been sleeping when they turned off the road, and his body desperately needed that chance to regain strength. But if he could identify whether they were going the right direction or not, they could get to the shelter of his brother's home far quicker. Of course, they couldn't see much for the snowfall that seemed to be growing thicker. Waking him might not help at all.

A bark sounded ahead, and she straightened, straining to see what Barney had spotted.

The dog stood at attention, staring through the snow. He barked again.

She reined in the mules lest they run over the mutt, for he hadn't left the center of the path.

Another figure appeared through the curtain of white. A man. Layered with such a thick coat and hood, she couldn't see much of him.

The stranger raised his hand toward her, maybe in greeting. As he walked by the dog, he held that arm out to Barney, but of course the animal slinked sideways out of reach.

As the man turned his focus on her and proceeded toward the side of the wagon, his gait turned wary. He halted a few steps away from the bench, his hood casting shadows over his eyes that made him look at least a score of years older than she. "Can I help you?"

She tightened her grip on the reins. Could he be dangerous? Aaron kept his rifle under the seat, but her hands were so cold, she might not be able to pull the trigger. Certainly not with any speed. Yet if Nate lived around here, this fellow could be a neighbor.

She lifted her voice. "We're looking for Nate Long's place. Do you know him?"

His gaze shot down the length of the wagon. "We?"

Better she make it clear she wasn't alone. "His brother's asleep in the wagon." Also better not to reveal Aaron's weakened condition.

But the stranger jerked into motion, striding toward the bed. "Aaron?"

Her heart hammered. This man knew him. He must not be a danger. She scrambled down from the wagon as the fellow moved to Aaron's blanket-wrapped body.

"Who are you?" She lifted her skirts and scrambled through the snow to catch up.

The man ignored her as he stared at the blanket-covered form. "Aaron?" He looked like he wasn't sure whether what lay beneath was a person or a viper that would spring up and bite him.

She reached the tailgate. "Who are you, sir?"

Still the man didn't answer, but he reached out and lifted an edge of the blanket.

The way he ignored her flared her anger. She grabbed his arm to pull it away, and he finally turned to her.

"I'm Nate Long. What's wrong with my brother?"

She tightened her grip. "You're Nate?" Now that he was closer, he didn't look as old as she'd first thought. The shadows must have added more grooves to his face than really existed.

She released his arm and turned to Aaron. "He's really sick. Has a broken leg and was kicked in the head, I think. He lay unconscious in the snow for a while before I found him. We've been driving for seven days to get him here to you."

Nate lifted the edge of the blanket again, a little higher this time so she could see Aaron's shadowed face too. His eyes were closed, his breathing ragged.

At least he *was* breathing. Her own inhales came faster.

"Brother, can you hear me?" Nate waited only a second before dropping the blanket and turning the direction he'd come from. "I'll get my horse and tell Laura. We have to take him to the doctor."

A weight lifted from her chest as she watched him sprint through the snow. She moved around to where she could lift the blanket to see Aaron's face. She used her thumb to stroke the side of his temple. "We're going to get you help, love. Hang on for me."

Tears stung her eyes, but then Aaron's lashes lifted. His weary gaze met hers, and though he didn't try to speak, she heard his meaning clearly. *Thank you. I love you.*

As his eyelids drifted closed again, she let the blanket rest and moved around to her seat on the bench. She had to be ready when Aaron's brother came back to lead them to the doctor.

~

"*A*re you sure neither of them is sick?" Aaron studied Doc Micah's familiar frank expression as the doctor rewrapped the splint around Aaron's leg.

"It's remarkable that baby stayed healthy, traveling in the cold and wind for so long. The covered bed you two made for her must have kept in her heat and blocked out the wind." Doc's eyes softened. "The Lord had all three of you safe under the shelter of His wing."

Aaron pushed a long breath out. "You're right about that." He glanced around the room, his old room where he'd spent so many long months. First, smothered by darkness. But then fighting to build up the strength in his leg. Laura had been his nurse, determined to see him recover. He'd been a louse through most of it, but eventually her tenacity had pushed him to try.

Leaving this room had given him the first real hope that he could find a normal life again. And now, being back here, lying in this bed with a splint strapping down one of his legs...

But he wasn't that old Aaron.

This wasn't a life-changing break, only a small fracture to the bone, as Micah called it. And he already had

God's promise of strength to keep him from succumbing to the darkness.

Not only that, but he had a precious gift—two precious gifts—lying in the room next door.

He looked back at the doctor. "Is this sickness contagious? Can I pass it to others?"

Doc shook his head. "The pneumonia's settled in your lungs, but it can't be spread at this point."

Aaron worked himself upright in the bed, then pulled the blanket off and reached for the walking sticks leaning against the chair. This old pair had been his companions for far too long, but he'd be thankful for them once again.

Doc Micah didn't try to stop him as he worked up to his feet, though that didn't surprise him. The doctor had always encouraged him to move around as much as he could during recovery.

It had been Aaron who'd resisted the pain of forcing himself to take action. But no longer. He needed to see his girls.

The door was closed to the room where Ingrid had said Katie was staying. Should he knock?

Of course he should. She wasn't his in full yet. But Lord willing, eventually, he would be able to claim the title of her husband.

Husband. He would have never thought he would be contemplating such. Once, he'd been one of the founding members of the toughest gang of thieves in the Montana territory. Yet now, he was not only contemplating marriage, he was *determined* to enter that state.

With Katie.

He tapped lightly on the door. No answer came. Was she up and around somewhere? She'd come to see him twice that he knew of, but he'd been so groggy, he could barely remember her visits. But that meant she had recovered enough from the journey she probably wasn't lying in bed all day.

Then a muffled voice sounded from inside. "Come in."

He turned the knob and nudged the door open.

Katie sat on the bed atop the covers, legs extended in front of her. Sarah lay in her lap, both tiny legs raised in the air. Katie had the babe's hands wrapped around her thumbs. The sight of the two of them there and the smile that bloomed across Katie's face sent a surge of warmth through his chest.

"Come see her. She's learning a new trick."

He hobbled forward with the walking sticks, and Katie tugged the chair beside her bed a little closer. He lowered into it, then leaned forward to see Sarah.

Her dark eyes scanned the ceiling, then landed on him.

"Hello, little girl. I think you grew while I slept."

She flapped one hand, almost as though she was reaching toward him.

"You think so too?" He slipped his finger against her palm, and she wrapped her tiny digits around his.

"See? That's her trick. She can hold onto your finger now." Katie's tone matched her smile, and he couldn't help grinning at her.

"She's a smart one, this girl." He almost said *our girl*, but he couldn't call her that yet. Not until Katie gave him permission.

Was it too soon to ask? He wanted so badly to let her know exactly how important she and Sarah had become to him.

He sat up and met Katie's gaze. "Katie, I—"

"Look who came to see you two."

A voice from the doorway interrupted his words, and he turned to see Mrs. Ingrid motioning to someone just outside. His chest squeezed with disappointment, but he tried to keep a pleasant expression.

Nate's head poked through the doorway, his teeth flashing in a grin. "You're alive." He directed that comment to Aaron, then shifted his focus to Katie. "Sorry to interrupt, ma'am. It's just good to finally see him up and around."

"Come in." Katie offered a welcoming smile. "Have you two had a chance to catch up yet?"

Nate stepped into the room, then motioned for someone still in the hallway. Laura edged in with him, and Nate drew her close with a hand at her waist. She looked uncertain, her gaze shifting between him and Katie.

But then her focus caught on Sarah. "Oh, look."

Katie turned her daughter so they could see, and Laura stepped closer.

"She's beautiful. And so tiny." She gave Katie a self-conscious smile. "I'm used to how big Micah and Ingrid's son William has grown. I forgot how small a newborn is."

Her voice shifted as she spoke directly to Sarah. "I'm not sure William was ever as tiny as you are, though."

"Would you like to hold her?" Katie's voice came softly.

An instinct in Aaron wanted to rise up and refuse. To keep Sarah protected in Katie's arms. But that was silly. Laura would be careful, and she deserved the chance to get to know this babe so important to him.

Laura took the infant gently, supporting her head as she laid her in the crook of her arm. "Look how precious you are." As she spoke to Sarah, she started a light rocking. "You barely weigh anything compared to William. I'll bet the two of you will be good friends."

The light brightening Laura's face reminded him of the day she'd married Nate. He glanced past her to his brother, and his besotted expression was hard to miss.

For the first time ever, Aaron could understand that feeling. His eyes traveled to Katie, who'd been watching Laura as she babbled to the babe. She must've felt his gaze, for she looked over at him, and the sweet smile curving her mouth made something in his chest flip.

He slid his hand across the blanket to wrap his fingers around hers. Even if he couldn't ask his question yet, just being with her was enough. And from the contentment in her eyes, maybe she felt the same way.

He gave her hand a light squeeze and shifted his focus back to Laura and the babe. But Nate caught his gaze instead.

His brother eyed him with raised brows and a quirk to his mouth. He shot a look down to where Aaron's hand joined Katie's. By the question in his eyes, he wanted to know exactly what was going on between them.

Aaron tried to shoot him a *mind your own affairs* glare, but the grin fighting hard at the corners of his mouth probably ruined the effect.

Nate's smirk took over and he gave a slight shake of his head, as though he'd known all along this would happen.

Aaron relaxed into his chair, letting himself fully enjoy being surrounded by these people he loved most —and who loved him. For the first time he could ever remember, he let himself soak in that love.

# EPILOGUE

"*H*ave you been back to the cave lately?" Aaron looked to his brother, who sat across the large kitchen table from him. They'd all gathered at Micah and Ingrid's home for a meal after church —his first time out of the clinic since arriving with Katie and Sarah.

The fact that he hadn't collapsed into bed as soon as they returned showed just how far he'd come in his recovery. The leg no longer ached all the time. The splint was more of a nuisance than anything. And his lungs didn't burn with each breath, though the cold winter air outside had made him cough again. Katie and the doctor had both insisted he bundle up tight, so the outing didn't feel like it caused any significant setback.

Good thing, for he wouldn't have wanted to miss this meal. They didn't often get to sit and visit together

—him and Katie, Nate and Laura, and Micah and Ingrid. Little William sat in a special chair their good friend Isaac had made for the boy, so the tot could be strapped in securely and have his own table tray in front of him.

As for Sarah, Aaron had taken her from Katie so she could help Ingrid and Laura with food preparations, and her little exhausted body had succumbed to exhaustion on his shoulder. She lay with her face near his neck, and her breaths tickled his skin, their sweet sound soothing his spirit.

Now, most of the food had been eaten, and he was simply enjoying the company.

In response to his question about the cave, Nate and Laura exchanged glances. Then his brother eyed him. "In fact, we have. We went by there a few weeks ago, and Bright Sun's entire family has come to winter in the large room where the hot springs run."

Laura leaned forward, her voice coming to life. "We got to meet her parents. And Eagle Soaring is still alive and seems well."

Aaron raised his brows. "That should be a nice protected place for them, if they can stand not having daylight."

Nate grimaced. "Don't I know it. But I think they're keeping cookfires going, so it's not bad. The hot spring keeps the cavern so warm, it's like summer in there, even with a blizzard blowing outside."

Silence settled over the group. Probably they were

remembering two winters ago when Nate and Laura had first discovered the cave, then found Bright Sun and her grandfather, Eagle Soaring, hiding within. The older man had been near death's door, and Bright Sun stood so brave to protect them both.

Or maybe they were remembering those men who'd kidnapped Bright Sun and Laura. The moment he'd realized what was happening, Aaron had known he'd had to be there for his brother. No matter how hard. That was the first time he'd left the doctor's clinic with the walking sticks, venturing to the livery to get a wagon so he could ride to the cave. And he'd made it just in time.

"I'll go lay Sarah down." Katie's quiet voice pulled him from the memories.

He met her gaze, and understanding glimmered there. He'd told her the story. He'd told her of that entire dark time and how God had used Laura and Nate and all these friends to pull him out. She'd also spoken of her life, of the dark days after leaving Pennsylvania. Of her time with her husband and how the man had died.

She'd spoken too of how she'd prayed for Aaron after his accident in the snow and on the journey to Settler's Fort. How she'd begun talking to God again, which she'd stopped doing years before. How a new hope was blooming inside her.

The one thing they hadn't spoken of was marriage.

For some reason, every time he'd started to ask her,

they'd been interrupted. Perhaps that was God's hand slowing him down, clamping his mouth shut until the right time.

As much as he'd rather not hand over Sarah, he allowed Katie to take her. But then he added, "I'll come with you," as he reached for his walking sticks. No matter how much time he spent with these two, he craved more. Even if that meant tagging along to help tuck the blanket around Sarah's sleeping form.

He caught Nate's knowing grin as he followed Katie from the room. But then William started babbling, and the conversation resumed around the boy's latest antics.

When they exited the doctor's private quarters into the wide hallway where patient rooms lined either side, Katie paused for him to come alongside her.

He hobbled as fast as he could without making too much racket with the poles on the wood floors. "I'll be glad when I can be done with these again."

She sent him a grin. "I read a passage in Romans earlier about suffering producing perseverance, which builds character, which strengthens our hope in God's love."

He gave her a look. She'd been reading the Bible? And memorizing it, too, apparently. He grinned. "I needed a reminder of that one. It's a verse I lean on for strength a lot."

She turned into her room and moved to the cradle Doc Micah had brought in for Sarah. William had grown out of it, and the scrollwork carved into the end panels seemed the perfect elegance for this sweet girl.

After Katie laid her down and tucked the blanket around her, she pressed a kiss to her fingers, then brushed them across Sarah's tuft of brown hair. He couldn't help tapping the end of the bundle where those little toes nestled. *Sleep well, my girl.*

Neither spoke until they left the room and Katie closed the door behind them. She moved against his side, and he wrapped his arms around her. He hadn't had the chance to hold her all day, and this felt like he'd finally come home.

He soaked in the sweet scent of her hair, its softness against his cheek. Thankfully, he'd shaved that morning before the service, so he had no whiskers to scratch her. Her body fit against his perfectly. Like they were made for each other.

He should ask her. Maybe this was finally the right time.

"Katie?"

"Hmm?" She pulled her head away from his shoulder to look at his face.

He loosened his grip but didn't let her go far. Someone would likely come along and interrupt them any second, but he wasn't letting go until he had to.

He studied her rich brown eyes, then raised a hand to stroke his thumb across her cheek. No woman had ever been as beautiful as she was, inside and out.

"The day I bought the freight wagon, I thought that

was my fresh start. My second chance at life, my way to show everyone the new man I was. The man God was growing me to be."

Her brow furrowed as she studied his face, listening with more than just her ears, but also with her heart and her own experiences.

He rested his fingers on her cheek, letting her warmth soak through him. "But I can see now all that was preparation for meeting you. So I could become the man you needed, along with God's help, of course. I've never, ever had the desire to marry. To settle in one place and be a family man. Not even when Nate did that very thing."

He did his best to show his heart in his eyes with this next part. "But you've changed all that. You and Sarah make me see life so differently than before. I'm not just existing anymore. Not just going from one day to the next. You make me smile from the moment I wake up. You give me something to look forward to, even if it's just holding that little girl in there while she sleeps."

Katie's mouth curved in her own sweet smile. A smile that made him want to lean in and taste those lips. To show her, not just tell, how much she meant to him.

But he hadn't gotten to the important part yet.

"Katie, I know you planned to go back to Philadelphia. To start fresh on your own back in the States. Do you think you could stand to have me alongside you? If you want to go to Pennsylvania, I'll find a way to support you there. Wherever you want to live, it would be my honor if you'd become my wife. Let me be a father to Sarah."

Her eyes shimmered, and her lower lip trembled a little. Was she going to cry? Did she mean to tell him no? Maybe that was why the Lord warned him off those other times. But why would God build this powerful love inside him, a love Aaron had certainly not planned for nor tried to grow?

Katie's arms around him tightened. Just a little, but enough to slow the racing in his chest. "Aaron, I don't care where I live anymore. Whether it be in Pennsylvania where I know, or this little haven of people who love you and have opened their arms to me. The one thing I do know is that you've claimed my heart more fully than I ever thought possible. And the way you love Sarah—" Her voice clogged with emotion, and she smiled through glassy eyes. She sniffed before continuing. "The way you love Sarah makes me love you all the more. We would both be overjoyed to be your girls."

His heart surged, nearly leaping from his chest. He clutched her closer, wrapping both arms tightly around her. If he could, he would spin her in a circle. But instead, he settled for pressing his mouth to hers.

She returned the kiss with enough fire to make his blood run hot. *Lord, only You could have blessed me so much more than I deserve.*

And he'd never take the blessing of this woman's love for granted. Not as long as he lived.

～

I pray you loved Aaron and Katie's story!
Would you like to receive a **free bonus epilogue with their wedding day and very first Christmas together?**
Get the bonus epilogue and sign-up for insider email updates at
https://mistymbeller.com/hmp-bonus-epilogue

～

*I*f you enjoyed this book, I think you'll also love *A Warrior's Heart*, book 1 in my Brides of Laurent series!

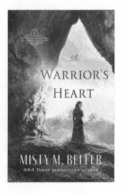

*𝒶* bout the book:
*Her heart longs for peace, but peace won't keep them safe.*

*Brielle Durand is still haunted by the massacre that killed her mother a dozen years before. Vowing to never let it happen again, she's risen to be the key defender for her people's peace-loving French settlement living in hidden caves in the Canadian Rockies. When a foreigner wanders too near to their secret home, she has no choice but to disarm and capture him. But now, what to do with this man who insists he can be trusted?*

*Hoping to escape past regrets, Evan MacManus ventured into the unknown, assigned to discover if the northern mountains contain an explosive mineral that might help America win the War of 1812. Despite being taken prisoner, Evan is determined to complete his mission. But when that assignment becomes at odds with his growing appreciation of the villagers and Brielle, does he follow through on his promise to his government or take a risk on where his heart is leading him? Either choice will cause harm to someone.*

*Brielle and Evan must reconcile the warring in their hearts to have any hope of finding peace for their peoples.*

Turn the page for a sneak peek at *A Warrior's Heart...*

# CHAPTER ONE

Rocky Mountains, Rupert's Land (Future Canada)

Another ten paces and she'd have to shoot.

Brielle Durand steadied the arrow fletching against her cheek, then pushed her body farther into the bow to draw the cord tighter.

The man in her sights rode calmly forward, his breath blowing white in the early morning air. The mount beneath him snorted, releasing its own cloud as it bobbed against the bit. The animal must sense the nearing danger.

In truth, the beast had more intelligence than its rider. As was usual in the ways of animals. Especially when compared to an Englishman like this fellow appeared to be.

Five more strides.

She narrowed her gaze, focusing on the point of aim so her arrow would hit his midsection. Should she give him warning? Perhaps the cry of a mountain lion would plant fear in his chest. She caught her breath, preparing to make the fierce scream she'd practiced so oft.

But the man spurred his horse faster, as though eager to charge through the opening in the rock. Surely he couldn't see the sheltered courtyard just beyond. The place forbidden to outsiders—especially Englishmen.

She locked her jaw to steady herself. Since her eighteenth birthday, when she'd finally been allowed to fight with the warriors, she swore an oath each morning to protect their village. Never again would an Englishman enter their inner circle unhindered. Her people had learned the terrible lesson well the last time. Memory of her mother's lifeless eyes tried to surface, but she pushed the distraction away.

Pressing against the bow, she took a final breath to aim, then let the arrow fly. *Guide its path, Lord.*

A roar broke the morning quiet, radiating from the rocky cliffs like the bellow of a wounded bear. The man doubled over, wrapping his arms around his middle. The long slender shaft of her arrow extended from the leathers that clothed him.

She inhaled a steadying breath, then released it. She'd done what she must to protect her people. Now came the time to uncover his reason for approaching the circle. Her home.

The safety of her people.

Evan McManus gripped the arrow shaft with both hands, forcing his body to draw in air despite the agony in his gut.

He'd not even heard the Indians' approach. Not noticed any quieting of the forest creatures. He must be losing his instincts, and this arrow served as grave proof of that fact.

He reined Granite into a cluster of trees, where the trunks might shield him from another arrow. Precious little time remained to extract the point before the Indians would be upon him. His hammering pulse only made each breath harder to inhale. He had to push aside the pain and focus on what must be done.

Feeling for the solid thickness of the arrowhead to make sure the iron hadn't sunk completely beneath his skin, he clenched his jaw at the cramping in his belly. Best to get this over with.

The arrow pulled loose from his flesh in a clean motion—maybe it hadn't sunk deep enough to damage any organs. The tip snagged on his buckskin tunic, and he wiggled it loose but stopped himself before hurling the wicked thing into the woods. With a hand pressing his undershirt against the wound to staunch the bleeding, he tucked the arrow in his musket scabbard and peered around the trunk of the tree nearest him. He could investigate which tribe had made the weapon later. If he survived this attack. At the moment, he had to find a way to ensure he didn't get a more personal introduction to whoever shot him.

No movement flashed in the morning light beyond the trees. Only a cluster of scraggly bushes marked the other side of the trail. But the warrior had likely been shooting from farther ahead, maybe even from the bend in the path, where the bases of two mountains met to form a narrow opening between them. The gap created a natural gateway where an enemy could find cover and wait.

A spasm seized Evan's belly, doubling him over as he fought to stifle a groan. He had to keep breathing, or this lightness in his head would take over.

"To the ground. Now," barked a voice behind him. The tone held an accent, but not any Indian tongue he'd ever heard.

Evan twisted, biting back a grunt as he tried to focus his wavering vision on the figure standing not five strides behind his horse, bow and arrow at the ready. He had no doubt that second arrow would find its way into his flesh if he didn't obey the order.

Pressing a hand tight against his wound, he clutched his saddle horn with the other and eased himself to the ground. He didn't release his hold on either the saddle or his gut as he tried to settle the spinning in his head. Had he lost so much blood already? The warm liquid coated his hand, which meant he wasn't staunching the flow. Yet he shouldn't be this lightheaded so quickly.

Ignoring the thought, he squinted at the bundle of furs before him.

"To the ground, I said. Or it's another arrow you'll meet."

That was no Indian's speech. Certainly not broken English, but the words contained a lilt only a Frenchman could master.

*Blast.* How had he stumbled upon the enemy all the way out here? He'd hoped—prayed—this territory was too far west for him to meet one of the Canadians they were fighting.

"Who are you?" He knew better than to argue with a man pointing a weapon, but the cramping in his gut made his thoughts swim in a disjointed flow.

A growl emanated from his adversary. Guttural, but not so deep as he would have expected. Still, the tone made it clear the fellow's patience was fast waning.

Evan released the saddle horn, lowered his arm, and sank to his knees on the frozen ground. Snow hadn't yet fallen in this part of the territory, but if the cold stinging his exposed skin was any indicator, an icy torrent would be upon them soon.

The Indian—or whoever was cloaked in the animal skins—circled around him, never dropping the aim of his arrow. The faint crackle of leaves bespoke an approach from behind. Would the man bind his wrists or pierce him with a knife and end his life?

Evan would have to turn and topple the stranger if he were to have any chance of getting the upper hand. He could do it, even with the arrow wound, certainly. He'd fought tougher opponents in battle after having received more than one slice from a saber. A

145

Frenchman would be an easy match—if only he could keep his swirling wits about him.

Footsteps padded behind him, and Evan tensed to spin and strike.

"Lower your—"

He whirled and shot his fist forward, praying his aim would be true, even though his target blurred into three shapes. His arm struck something—fur?—and the man issued a high-pitched gasp. Was this a boy?

But Evan had no time to ponder as something grabbed his wrist and a force slammed into his back, shoving him down, almost to the ground.

He writhed, jerking his arm to get away from the man's grasp. Evan brought his free hand around to strike a blow. The effort sent a knife of pain through his gut, but he clamped his jaw tight and fought harder.

His opponent moved too quickly, out of striking distance before Evan could land a blow. His dizziness must be slowing his movements, but he had to overcome that. The man had Evan's arm pinned behind him now, and a boot in his back, pressing him toward the dirt.

He resisted the pressure, his belly hovering about a foot above the forest floor. But the effort stole his strength more every second. He'd have enough energy left for one more counterattack, and this time he had to overcome his enemy or he'd never complete his mission. He'd already spotted signs that he might have reached his goal.

This mountain he'd been riding around possessed the orange striations usually found near pitchblende. Now, he had to locate that mineral itself so the Army's scientists could create the blast that would finally end this brutal war. This work was all he had left, and he'd carry out his assignment no matter what it took.

Somehow, he had to make restitution for last time.

With a mighty effort, he twisted around, reaching for the ankle that held him low. The attacker must have been prepared for his movement and grabbed Evan's free wrist, jerking his hand upward so his arms burned at the joint of his shoulders—effectively stealing the last of his strength and gaining the upper hand. Literally.

Were these his final moments? They couldn't be. *God, help me.*

Evan knelt there, struggling for breath. Even when he sucked in air, the wind didn't seem to satisfy the craving in his chest. Perhaps the arrow had punctured his breathing vessel.

His captor worked quickly with his wrists, wrapping a rough cord around them. Despite the unsteadiness in his head, Evan strained to look around, to keep his ears aware of any sound that might give notice of more enemies approaching. Perhaps help, even, as unlikely as that was. But one could hope.

No unnatural noises greeted him. Only a pheasant's call broke the cold silence.

At last, the man behind him gave a final jerk on the binding, then released Evan's hands. The immediate relief in his upper arms seemed to sap a little more of his strength as his body sagged.

"You will walk." The man's voice had such an unusual accent, making it hard to place either his age or nationality. Definitely young, though.

How humbling. Here he was, Evan McManus, former captain in the American army and now a trusted spy commissioned by President Madison himself, brought down by a lad with a bow and arrow.

Evan struggled to his feet, spreading them wide to keep from toppling over as his vision swam. Even with his eyes squeezed tight, his body wobbled more than he could control. He shouldn't be this affected by a simple wound, even with the blood loss. Had the arrowhead been tainted? He'd heard tales of Indians dipping the tips in poison before battle.

A hand gripped his arm, giving him something to brace against—until it yanked him forward. Still, the hold kept him upright as he forced one foot in front of the other. The grip felt small, even through the layers of his coat.

Evan forced his eyes open, but the sunlight made the dizziness more intense. He tried squinting, which helped. He had to stay alert, watch his surroundings if he was going to get out of this alive. So far, they appeared to be walking the same path north he'd been riding. Toward the opening between the mountains.

When they reached the spot, his captor loosed a piercing whistle. Evan fought to keep from cringing at the surprise blast so near his ear, but a fresh blade of pain pierced his middle anyway. When a second shrill whistle came, he almost jabbed the lad with his elbow.

But the reply that sounded from the other side of the rock grabbed his focus. They wove around a boulder to proceed through the opening, and Evan squinted again now that he could see bright daylight on the other side.

The place looked to be a meadow of sorts. With figures darting through the winter brown grass. Voices called, or maybe laughed. Children's voices? The pain and blood loss must be making him daft. Or maybe he was being taken to an Indian village. He had to stay awake and watch for a chance to escape.

His captor pushed him forward as other figures approached. These, too, were wrapped in animal skins, but their bulk proved them to be full-grown men. His vision blurred further, even when he tried to focus. He couldn't make out much more than dark or light hair.

Low murmurings sounded around him, yet they seemed to come from so far away. Or maybe it was he who had moved. He had to recover his strength. Squinting again, he tried to straighten. "Who are you?"

The talking around him ceased, and a figure stepped in front of him. He blinked to focus, and the fur cloaking the person began to look familiar. His captor.

The man reached up and pushed the hood off his head, revealing dark hair and a smooth face.

Evan blinked. He must be dafter than he realized,

although with the person less than a stride away, it was hard to miss what his eyes took in.

*A woman?*

Even through his shadowy vision, he could make out the delicate angles of her face. Those piercing dark eyes.

"You have come to Laurent. Now you will tell us why." The lilt in her voice sounded different now that he could see her. With her tone so melodic, how could he not have recognized her as female?

A fresh wave of dizziness washed over him, and he braced his feet. A hand gripped his arm, that same small hand as before.

"Your purpose, monsieur. Before you swoon, if you please."

Even if he wanted to tell her, his mouth had turned to cotton. Blackness circled the edge of his vision, increasing until he could only see her blurry form through a small hole, as though looking through a field glass. This lightness in his head almost took over completely. His body sank like it weighed twice as much as usual.

*Lord, don't let them kill me. Not yet.*

He had too much to make up for. Too much left to fix before he faced the final judgment.

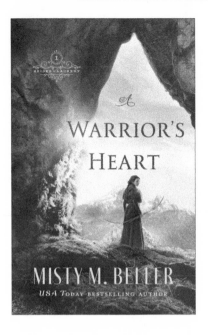

Get A Warrior's Heart at your favorite retailer!

Did you enjoy Aaron and Katie's story? I hope so!
**Would you take a quick minute to leave a review
where you purchased the book?**
It doesn't have to be long. Just a sentence or two telling
what you liked about the story!

To receive a free book and get updates when new Misty
M. Beller books release, go to <u>https://mistymbeller.com/
freebook</u>

# ALSO BY MISTY M. BELLER

**The Mountain Series**

The Lady and the Mountain Man

The Lady and the Mountain Doctor

The Lady and the Mountain Fire

The Lady and the Mountain Promise

The Lady and the Mountain Call

This Treacherous Journey

This Wilderness Journey

This Freedom Journey (novella)

This Courageous Journey

This Homeward Journey

This Daring Journey

This Healing Journey

**Call of the Rockies**

Freedom in the Mountain Wind

Hope in the Mountain River

Light in the Mountain Sky

Courage in the Mountain Wilderness

Faith in the Mountain Valley

Honor in the Mountain Refuge

Peace in the Mountain Haven

Grace on the Mountain Trail

Calm in the Mountain Storm

**Brides of Laurent**

A Warrior's Heart

A Healer's Promise

A Daughter's Courage

**Hearts of Montana**

Hope's Highest Mountain

Love's Mountain Quest

Faith's Mountain Home

**Texas Rancher Trilogy**

The Rancher Takes a Cook

The Ranger Takes a Bride

The Rancher Takes a Cowgirl

**Wyoming Mountain Tales**

A Pony Express Romance

A Rocky Mountain Romance

A Sweetwater River Romance

A Mountain Christmas Romance

# ABOUT THE AUTHOR

**Misty M. Beller** is a *USA Today* bestselling author of romantic mountain stories, set on the 1800s frontier and woven with the truth of God's love.

Raised on a farm and surrounded by family, Misty developed her love for horses, history, and adventure. These days, her husband and children provide fresh adventure every day, keeping her both grounded and crazy.

Misty's passion is to create inspiring Christian fiction infused with the grandeur of the mountains, writing historical romance that displays God's abundant love through the twists and turns in the lives of her characters.

Sharing her stories with readers is a dream come true for Misty. She writes from her country home in South Carolina and escapes to the mountains any chance she gets.

**Connect with Misty at <u>www.MistyMBeller.com</u>**